KU-488-121

CAPTAIN W. E. JOHNS

ORCHIDS FOR BIGGLES

KNIGHT BOOKS
the paperback division of Brockhampton Press

ISBN 0 340 19620 3

This edition first published 1975 by Knight, the
paperback division of Brockhampton Press, Leicester.
First published 1962 by Brockhampton Press Ltd

Text copyright © 1962 Capt. W. E. Johns

Printed and bound in Great Britain by
Cox & Wyman Ltd, London, Reading and Fakenham

Colin's

ORCHIDS FOR BIGGLES

Top secret documents are missing and with
them a nuclear research scientist demanding
one million dollars for the return of the
papers which in enemy hands could only
mean annihilation. Biggles and Bertie try
to track down Harald Neckel in the
Peruvian jungle – and Bertie's struggle
with a giant anaconda is by no means their
closest brush with death.

CONTENTS

PREFACE

Here are some explanatory notes about the family of plants known as Orchidaceae, *or Orchids*

THE orchid family is a peculiar race of plants, most of which, in nature, occur in tropical countries, although a few of no account do grow in temperate zones, including the British Isles. There are about five hundred altogether, divided into two groups: Terrestrial, that is those which have roots in the ground, and Epiphytic, meaning a plant which grows on another, often with air roots, deriving moisture from the atmosphere. These usually spring from thick bulbous roots called pseudo-bulbs. Some are useless for any purpose, but others, by virtue of the beauty of their flowers, have a high commercial value. One or two have other properties, such as *vanilla,* the seed pods of which yield the well-known flavouring substance of that name.

The culture of exotic orchids in temperate climates necessitates a hothouse, but even so, as many types demand their own highly specialised conditions of temperature, moisture, light and shade, to grow them successfully calls for understanding, skill and patience; which is why they are so expensive. Another reason for this is, the seeds are microscopic and delicate, and to produce a flowering plant from seed generally takes several years of exceptionally careful cultivation.

Bulbs are sometimes imported from the country of origin, either to the order of professional growers or for sale at public auctions.

W.E.J.

CHAPTER 1

THE ORCHID MAN

THE rain was not particularly heavy, but it dropped straight down from an unbroken layer of cloud, the colour of lead, with relentless persistence, getting no heavier yet giving no indication of ending. It splashed with a constant hiss on the black water of the Rio Jurara and bounced off the plane surfaces of the Air Police amphibious aircraft 'Gadfly' which, with engines idling, rested on the river, drifting a little under the weight of storm water already pouring into the main stream from a thousand minor tributaries.

There was no wind; no movement of air. The great trees of the Amazonian forest that lined the banks appeared, on the near side, as a cliff of dark grey rock, and the other as a vague shadow that merged into the sky.

Biggles eyed the rising water with misgivings. Already it was bringing down from the upper reaches the usual miscellaneous debris, broad masses of weed, dead trees and the like. On one such precarious raft a monkey chattered with rage at finding itself so trapped.

A dugout canoe went past, a blanket-shrouded figure hunched in the stern trailing a paddle.

Biggles opened the streaming cabin window a little

9

way to inspect more easily a large, palm-thatched house, that stood on stilts beyond a beach of coal-black mud up which the rising flood was creeping.

'This could be it,' he said, to his only companion in the aircraft, Air-Constable Bertie Lissie. 'I hope to goodness it is, because we can't go on like this. If we take off, with visibility as it is we might have a job to get down again; and if we stay where we are we're liable to get a hole punched in our hull by one of these logs I see being washed down.'

Bertie took a look at the house through the open window. 'I'd hardly call that place a villa, old boy,' he observed seriously.

'We're not in the South of France,' Biggles reminded him. 'What did you expect to find – a row of marble pillars and a flight of steps sweeping up to the front door?'

'I certainly didn't expect to strike this sort of weather,' complained Bertie. 'I thought we were coming to the tropics. Dash it all, I've brought my Bombay bowler*.'

'You may need it yet. It has to rain sometimes even in the tropics. The sky isn't blue all the time.'

'So I notice,' returned Bertie. 'What can we do about it?'

'Nothing.'

'How long is this bally downpour likely to last?'

'Don't ask me. I wouldn't know. But I do know this. Sitting here goofing at it won't get us anywhere. I'm going ashore to ask if this is Fotherham's place. If it

* Pith helmet

isn't, someone might be able to tell us where it is. My information was, Fotherham lived up a creek about four miles downstream from Cruzuado, and that, as near as I can judge in the foul murk, is where we are. Here, take the stick and run me in close. Go steady. I imagine the bottom will be mud, but I'm taking no chances of tearing our keel off on an odd rock or a sunken tree.'

Bertie complied, and the aircraft nosed its way cautiously to the beach until the keel scraped gently on a soft bottom.

Biggles stepped out into several inches of evil-smelling sludge and walked on, with his feet sinking in sticky mud, towards the house. Before he reached it he observed that he was being watched by several pairs of eyes, mostly Indian; but a man who must have been sitting on the veranda, and now came forward to meet him, was obviously a half-caste.

As a specimen of the human race he was far from perfect. Bearded and indescribably filthy, he wore only three articles of clothing; a battered slouch hat, a shirt in tatters open to the waist, and a pair of baggy canvas trousers supported by a leather belt through which had been thrust, without any protection, a heavy knife. However, he answered Biggles cheerfully enough when he greeted him with the usual *'Buenos dias, señor,'* adding *'Que mal tiempo.'* (What bad weather.)

'El tiempo esta muy insequro,' (the weather is very unsettled) the man announced, somewhat unnecessarily.

Ignoring what seemed a nice piece of understatement Biggles walked on with the man to the shelter under the house, where a pile of rough balls of crude rubber suggested the man was a trader in that commodity, and proceeded with the question he had come to ask. It turned out that the man had had an English father, or so he claimed, and as he spoke English fairly well it could have been true. This made conversation easier.

No, the man told him, this was not the Villa Vanda of Señor Fotherham, whom he knew well, often doing business with him in orchids which his men found in the forest when tapping the wild rubber trees. The villa was on the same bank about a mile higher in a little creek. As soon as the creek was entered the house of Don Pedro would be seen on the right.

Biggles, having got the information he wanted, declined with thanks an invitation to enter the house for a meal and returned to the beach and so into the aircraft.

'We're only about a mile short of Fotherham's place so we haven't done too badly,' he told Bertie. 'It's up a creek. We're on the right side of the river so let's press on.'

'Do you want me to take off?'

'No. It isn't worth it. We might as well stay on the water. Take it slowly and keep an eye open for timber floating down. I'll watch for the creek.'

Bertie turned the bows of the Gadfly into the current and the machine forged its way forward with Biggles peering through the open window for the creek described by the amiable rubber trader.

A few minutes later they came to it, finding it without difficulty as the man had promised, for the gap in the bank was fairly wide and gave entrance to a sheet of placid water in the manner of a long, narrow lake. A house came into view on the right-hand side. It still fell far short of the establishment which the name, Villa Vanda, suggested. Indeed, it appeared to be little better than the house just visited. It was a little larger and could boast some extensive outbuildings; but its general appearance was just as untidy. A pier, or landing stage, of rough timber, ran out a short distance into the water. Tied up to it were two exceptionally large canoes and a balsa – a raft of very light wood used largely in the Amazon Basin. Some Indians who had been working on these craft stopped what they were doing to watch the aircraft as it drew near.

'You're not going to tell me that an Englishman, with a university education behind him, lives in that miserable-looking barn,' remarked Bertie.

'Englishmen have lived in worse places than that,' returned Biggles. 'Where people choose to live is a matter of taste, and considering how long he's been here Fotherham must like it.'

'I'll bet the place is crawling with fleas.'

'I shall be surprised if there aren't worse pests than fleas living in that thatch,' rejoined Biggles cheerfully. 'It's ready made for all sorts of little beasts that bite and sting. However, we don't have to live in it. I imagine we shall find the hotel in the town not too bad.'

'I hope you're right, old boy,' answered Bertie fervently. 'Pity we couldn't have gone straight to it. I'm all for hot and cold laid on. One needs a bath three times a day in this climate.'

'You know why we couldn't do that. The machine would have attracted too much attention. I want to arrive with as little fuss as possible. I'm hoping Fotherham, or Don Pedro as they call him, will allow us to park the aircraft here. He'll have servants to keep an eye on it. That would enable us to proceed on foot. There's bound to be a track to Cruzuado, if not a road.'

'What if he invites us to stay here with him?'

'I'm keeping an open mind about that. It may suit us for a day or two until we see how the land lies. I'm not particular about what the house is like inside as long as there's a roof over our heads to keep off this infernal rain.'

'If I know anything about jungle paths it's not going to be fun padding the hoof between here and Cruzuado in this sort of weather. I don't know about you, but I'm not finding it any too warm in tropical kit. I should have kept on my woollies.'

'You'll find it hot enough when the sun breaks through,' promised Biggles. 'This rain is coming from the west, which means the clouds have been in touch with the snow and ice on the high tops of the Andes. That's why it's a bit chilly. It'll improve.'

'It can't get much worse, there is that about it,' observed Bertie.

By this time the aircraft had touched its nose against an unoccupied part of the pier so Biggles got out and made fast. Bertie, having switched off, joined him, observing that a man, a white man, was walking quickly from the house to meet them; they went on and presently came face to face with him.

'Mr Peter Fotherham?' questioned Biggles.

'At your service,' was the reply.

Biggles' eyes made a quick survey of the speaker, and what he saw he found embarrassing if not disconcerting. Fotherham was so casual as to be almost shabby. It would have been difficult to guess his age, but making allowances for his physical condition Biggles judged him to be in the region of forty. He was tall, and thin to the point of emaciation. His skin, the colour of old parchment from recurrent fever or jaundice, appeared to be stretched over a framework of bones. His face was long and narrow with a high forehead and a prominent jaw. But blue eyes, and reddish unkempt hair beginning to turn grey, left no doubt about European descent. The hand that he offered to them in turn was not that of a man accustomed to manual labour.

He did not wear much in the way of clothes, although he could have claimed with truth that in the usual sultry heat of his chosen place of residence he needed no more than was necessary to cover his nakedness. He wore a much-worn khaki cotton shirt, drill shorts of the same colour and a pair of mud-caked plimsolls. When he spoke it was with the voice of a man of culture.

'Welcome to Vanda,' he said. 'I seldom have visitors so you must be Bigglesworth and Lissie. I was informed you were coming. Did you have much difficulty in finding me?'

'I had a job to find the right river, never mind your house,' answered Biggles, smiling. 'It was easy to Manicore, and for some way afterwards, because we followed the local air service to Porto Velho; but when we struck the tangle of rivers you have about here it wasn't easy to follow the right one. However, after landing once or twice to ask the way we've managed to get here.'

'Good. That's the main thing. Come up to the house and have a drink. You might like to take a bath and change your clothes. My men will bring your luggage along.'

'Will my aircraft be all right?'

'As right as rain, as we might say, not inappropriately. There's no current to speak of in the creek and my men wouldn't interfere with it.'

The little party walked towards the house, across the front of which, as could now be seen, had been nailed a board carrying the words, in faded letters: '*Peter Fotherham. Orchids.*' As if to emphasise the point, from it hung a big wire basket carrying a magnificent orchid, ablaze with blue and lilac flowers.

Fotherham pointed to it. 'Do you know what that is?'

Biggles answered. 'No beyond the fact that it's an orchid.'

'Quite right. It's one of the family Vanda – hence the name of my house. It's a type that doesn't occur here. I raised it myself from seed. I raise quite a few hybrids, apart from what are collected in the forest.'

They were now splashing through a yard where, in a strong smell of chemicals, several Indians, negroes and mixed breeds, were busy with piles of orchid bulbs, some bearing exquisite flowers which were being torn off and thrown down in the mud before the bulbs were tossed into a large vat.

'Sorry to bring you through all this mess but some of my collectors have just brought in their loads,' said Fotherham apologetically.

'Then you don't go out looking for them yourself,' said Bertie.

'I used to, but not now,' replied Fotherham. 'I only go out when I receive a report of something special that might require careful handling. I'm not as young as I was and you have to be a Tarzan to climb the trees and bring down the bulbs. Like everything else, the value of orchids is determined by rarity, and the business of handling them is not as simple as you might imagine. It isn't just a matter of finding, collecting, and packing the stuff off home. Few countries will permit the import of orchid roots in the rough state for fear of introducing some dangerous pest. They have to be cleaned and treated with chemicals to rid them of worms and bugs, even small snakes and tarantulas, that make their homes in them. That's what those fellows in the yard are doing now.'

'What I don't understand is why it's necessary to import bulbs at all,' said Biggles. 'Can't enough be raised in hothouses at home to satisfy the demand?'

'You can do that for so long,' informed the specialist. 'Bred in captivity, so to speak, after a while the stock loses its stamina and the flowers their perfume, so it's necessary from time to time to bring in new blood to renew their strength by the introduction of healthy stock direct from the forest.'

'What started you off in this unusual line of business?' inquired Biggles. 'You've been at it for a long time, I believe.'

'I collect orchids chiefly for myself, and supply other people, not because I need the money, but because I love the flowers for themselves and am in the fortunate position of being able to indulge in a hobby which most people would find too expensive. It's not uncommon for a person to be struck with a passion for collecting. It may be postage stamps, or fossils, or even matchbox tops. With me it is orchids. Many years ago, when I came down from Oxford, my father gave me the money for a world tour, and it was in Burma that I saw my first wild orchid, *Vanda Caerulescens* – one of the parents of the one you saw outside. I had always been a naturalist and I thought I had never seen anything as lovely as that blue orchid. My father died shortly after I returned home, so finding myself well off I was able to indulge in the luxury of building up a collection of orchids. Then came the war. One frosty night my glasshouses were shattered in an accident and by morning my collection had ceased to exist. It had died from cold. Determined to see that should never happen again, as soon as the war was over I came here, where no artificial heat is necessary; and here I've been ever since.'

They had now entered what was obviously the living room, a long apartment simply but comfortably furnished, mostly in bamboo, presumably of local manufacture. There were some metal cabinets against one wall. The decorations consisted chiefly of glass cases containing specimens of gorgeous birds and butterflies.

'What would you like to drink?' inquired Fotherham, going to a table on which stood bottles and glasses.

'Whisky – gin? Or would you rather have something soft?'

'I see you have some lime juice there,' answered Biggles. 'I keep off alcohol in hot climates.'

'Very wise,' agreed the orchid man. 'I'm sorry about the stink. One soon gets used to it. I have to use a strong insect repellant to protect my collection of butterflies and moths.'

'Do you live here alone?' asked Biggles, as he accepted his drink.

'Yes, except for servants, mostly Indians I've trained. My cook, Gaspard, is half French, and he looks after me very well. A good negro is boss of the yard. I've no women about the place. They cause more trouble than they're worth. By the way, to everyone in the district I'm known as Don Pedro. I'm afraid they all think I'm a bit mad.' Fotherham laughed. 'Perhaps they're right. Here they have a saying that everyone is mad except yourself.'

'Don't you ever feel like going home?' asked Bertie.

'No. That's a thing of the past. I've been here too long to change my way of life. I like it here, and if you have what you like, why change? I have none of the worries and irritations that affect people in what is called civilisation. What can't be done today can be done tomorrow, or the next day, or next week – or never. It doesn't matter. The jungle has that effect on you. It either kills you or makes you its slave for life. I couldn't do without it now. As a boy I was fascinated by natural history, and here I am always finding something new to marvel at.'

Biggles smiled. 'Well, if you like jungle you've certainly got plenty of it.'

'You're right there,' agreed Fotherham. 'From the mouth of the Amazon to Iquitos in Peru the distance is nearly three thousand miles, and it's jungle on both banks for most of the way. Mind you, I'm not alone in liking this sort of life. The country is full of people from Europe, refugees, displaced persons, to say nothing of criminal fugitives from justice. They all hope to make a quick fortune in gold, diamonds, emeralds or what have you, but they seldom succeed. They always intend to go home, and are for ever talking about it, but they rarely go. Usually they run out of money and, unable to pay the fare, they have to stay, whether they like it or not. Now tell me. What are you gentlemen going to do? What exactly was your purpose in coming here? I was advised by my London agents that you were on your way, but the reason was not made clear.'

Biggles answered. 'Between ourselves we represent an organisation in England that is now taking a particular interest in this part of the world. We're here to explore certain possibilities which at the moment I'm not at liberty to discuss. I may be able to tell you more when we've had a look round.'

'Then it isn't entirely orchids you're after?'

'No. To be frank, orchids were really an excuse, so we shall at least have to pretend we're interested in them. In other words, they provided a convenient reason for our being here. We were given your name because it was thought you'd be able to advise us on such things as

local administration, and possibly give us a hand should
we run into trouble.'

'I see. Well, I shall be happy to do what I can. I can
give you a shakedown here if you care to stay.'

'That's most kind of you, but we wouldn't think of
trespassing on your hospitality,' answered Biggles. 'Our
intention, having made ourselves known to you, was to
find accommodation in Cruzuado, which I understand is
quite close. We were given the name of a hotel – the
Comisaria.'

'That's probably the best place, although it isn't really
what you'd call a hotel by European standards. It's more
of a *posada*, that is, an inn. I'm well known to the
patron. I looked in the last time I was in town, about a
week ago, and found myself talking to another new arrival, a Russian, I believe.'

Biggles looked up sharply. 'Oh, and what's he doing
here?'

'I have no idea. He didn't volunteer the information
and here it's considered impolite to ask personal questions.'

'What sort of place is Cruzuado?' queried Biggles,
thinking it imprudent to press the subject of the Russian
visitor, which was of more interest to him.

'You'll find it a bit rough, and considering where we
are you'd hardly expect anything else,' replied Don
Pedro.

'There's little serious police control, although to be
sure the *Intendente* does all he can to keep order; but for
a place like this he's hopelessly understaffed. A man is
expected to be able to take care of himself. The local

people, storekeepers or traders in one line or another, are all right. So are the Indians, negroes and mixed breeds who work for them. The trouble is mostly caused by the *llaneros,* cowboys if you like, who come in, usually at weekends, for a spree. They work on the open plains beyond the forest belt, where beef cattle are raised. They come in simply to get drunk on beer or the local spirit called *Aguardiente,* and there are plenty of bars and dance halls to cater for them. Or they may go to the cinema to jeer at the latest nonsense from civilisation. But the town is now reasonably safe for visitors, which is more than could be said for it when I first came here.'

'So there's a cinema?'

'Of sorts. I'd advise you not to go near it. It's not uncommon for a film to end with empty bottles being thrown at the screen. Rows in which shooting and knifings occur are not uncommon. Nobody bothers. If there's a policeman about he keeps out of the way. Monday morning usually finds the town in a stupor, sleeping off the effects of the night before. I don't go in more than is absolutely necessary.'

'Not exactly a health resort,' put in Bertie.

'Anything but that. It isn't a pretty place. Cheapness being the first consideration the houses are mostly what here is called *tapial,* which is mud and chopped grass pounded together in a long mould. The bricks are made in position and holes afterwards knocked through where the windows are to be. A coat of whitewash and that's it. Sanitation is practically nonexistent.'

'I take it there's a road from here to the town?' asked Biggles.

'Call it a track. You won't find it easy going in any conditions, let alone after all this rain. I suggest you stay here for the night, or until the rain stops. Tomorrow it may be fine. I can lend you ponies and a guide to show you the way. You can keep the ponies in Cruzuado in case you decide to come back here.'

'That's very kind of you,' said Biggles. 'We're most grateful. But wouldn't it be easier to travel by the river? The town stands on the river, I believe.'

'I wouldn't try it with this storm water coming down. There are too many hazards to make the risk worth while. You'll find it easier, and safer, to travel overland. Your plane will be all right here. I'll keep an eye on it. But it's time you had something to eat. Let's go through to the dining room. Afterwards, if you'd care to see it, I'll show you my orchid garden. I have some very rare specimens which you're not likely to see elsewhere.'

'Thanks. As we're supposed to be in the orchid business we'd better learn something about them,' said Biggles.

'You'd better learn something about the river, too. It's practically impossible to travel against the current when it's like this, or at any time after a lot of rain. That Russian I spoke about had had his plan upset. He took a passage for Cruzuado on one of the wood-burning ferry steamers, but owing to the head of water it couldn't get beyond Puerto Vecho, about twenty miles downstream from here, so he had to complete his journey overland. And while we're on the subject of the river, keep out of the water if you can. The Jurara has a bad name for *tembladores*.'

'What are they?'

'Electric eels. They can knock a horse over, never mind a man.'

'I'll bear it in mind,' promised Biggles, as they followed their host into the next room.

CHAPTER 2

THE TRAITOR

Now let us turn back the clock for ten days to discover the reason for Biggles' sudden interest, or to be honest, pretended interest, in the most exotic, and perhaps the most beautiful, flowers in the world.

It all began one morning when his chief, Air Commodore Raymond of the Special Air Police, buzzed him on the intercom telephone to call him to his office immediately.

Biggles answered the call.

'Pull up a chair,' ordered the Air Commodore. 'This is going to take a little while so relax and help yourself to cigarettes.'

'Judging from your expression, sir, there's something in the offing with an offensive aroma,' observed Biggles as he complied.

'It stinks,' returned the Air Commodore, succinctly. 'When I say a thing is serious you know what that means. To get the trouble ironed out without raising a howl that might echo round the world is going to call for the last word in delicate handling.'

'Sounds like something political,' surmised Biggles, his eyes on his chief's face.

'I suppose you could call it that within the small circle

25

of people who know about it. It's top level secret. If one whisper leaks out the armchair critics who jump at any excuse to have a smack at the government are likely to break out in a rash.'

Biggles frowned. 'I hate these jobs. If they work out all right that's the last we hear of it. If anything comes unstuck we get the dirty end of the stick.'

'If this one comes unstuck the government will disclaim all knowledge of the matter.'

'And we take the rap.'

'Of course. Still, to be fair we've been offered every possible facility. Money is no object. All that matters is we succeed in what is – let's face it – one of the stickiest assignments that have come our way.'

'What is this, then? Espionage?'

'No. Blackmail.'

'Who's blackmailing whom?'

'The blackmailer is an individual named Harald Neckel, and the party being blackmailed is the British Government – no less.'

'Stiffen the crows! This is a new idea.'

'New and nasty. It's no use trying to deceive ourselves. It's within the power of this rogue Neckel to do so much mischief that it doesn't bear thinking about. Not only could he rock our reputation internationally, but the arguments and recriminations that would follow exposure would tear this country wide open. The government has enough troubles already. The trouble is, Neckel is no ordinary criminal. We're up against a man with an exceptional brain.'

'What does he want?'

'Money.'

'Then why not give him the money and have done with it?'

'It isn't as easy as that, as you'll realise when you've heard the whole story.'

'What nationality is this crook?'

'On his own word, and to the best of our knowledge, he's a Rumanian – or was, until he became a naturalised British subject five years ago. I'd better start by giving you his background, as we understand it, because that will enable you to grasp more easily a curious factor in the position as it stands today.'

Biggles nodded and settled down to listen.

'Neckel was born in Lima, Peru, forty-four years ago, of Rumanian parents. His father was a civil servant in the service of the Rumanian government. Note that from starting life in South America Neckel speaks the local Spanish like a native. At the age of twelve he was sent to school in the United States, where he learned to speak English with a slight American accent. Shortly after he returned home – that is, to Lima – his father was recalled to Rumania, and the family then resided in Bucharest. There Neckel continued his studies. The intention was he should enter the diplomatic service, but having a remarkable aptitude for figures he switched to science, in which subject he took a degree and in due course became a Professor at the University. Later, not liking the atmosphere behind the Iron Curtain, or thinking possibly his prospects were better here, he got under the Curtain and came over to the West. I'll now proceed to the present situation.'

'How did he get into a position to be able to dictate to us?'

'I'm coming to that. The story isn't unique. It has happened before more than once. Unfortunately, no matter what the job may be, somebody has to trust somebody, and that applies to top secret work as much as to any normal occupation. We trusted this man. We had to. Other men we have trusted have let us down, and that, as you may recall, does not exclude British born subjects. But in all previous cases when a man has absconded he was influenced chiefly, if not entirely, by politics. That is to say, he has been induced to take up communism and so disappear into Eastern Europe. That has operated both ways, of course. Just as many men, if not more, have slipped through the Iron Curtain to come over to the West.'

'Then Neckel hasn't gone to Russia?'

'No. That is, as far as we know, not yet. He seems to be the exception who isn't interested in politics. He's only concerned with himself, and money. But let me give you a quick outline of events here, which began twelve years ago when a man arrived in this country asking for political asylum. His name, he said, was Harald Neckel, a Professor of Science who had been working in Bucharest. In view of the ability he was soon to demonstrate there seemed no reason to doubt this. He declared he had never liked communism, that he now found it intolerable, and so had come to this country hoping to get a job in one of our research establishments. Tested for ability he was found to be a mathe-

matical genius, one of those rare creatures that think
only in terms of figures.'

'Coming from where he did, that alone wouldn't be
enough to get him a job in one of our secret depart-
ments, I imagine,' put in Biggles.

'Of course not. The security people got busy on him,
checking on his past, and while they didn't learn much,
what they did find out fitted with what Neckel had told
them. Anyway, exhaustive inquiries revealed nothing
against him, so for a start he was given a minor position
in one of our research laboratories, with security officers
still keeping a watchful eye on him. He settled down in
his work, to which he seemed dedicated, and not by
word or action did he make a move that could in any
way be regarded as suspicious. The result was that
after two years security precautions were relaxed
somewhat and he was promoted to a position for
which the qualifications he had revealed made him
suitable. As time went on he continued to improve
until he became one of our top men in nuclear research.'

'And all this time his behaviour had been exemp-
lary.'

'Yes. And let us admit it, after twelve years of excellent service, security arrangements had been almost
withdrawn altogether. In other words, he was considered safe.'

'Yet he turned out to be a spy after all?'

'Yes and no. That is, not in the generally accepted
sense of the term, in that he was working for a foreign
power. He still appeared to have no interest whatever in

politics; and what he has done now has no political bias.'

'Then who was he working for?'

'Himself.'

'What has he done?'

'He's cleared off.'

'Does that matter so much? You managed without him before he came to this country.'

'As a person he isn't vital, although his loss would be felt in the department in which he has been working. It's the old story. He asked for leave of absence to take a holiday. As this was certainly long overdue the request was granted. He didn't return. All trace of him was lost. Not unnaturally we supposed he had skipped back behind the Iron Curtain, but even there our agents could get no news of him. Whether what he has done had been in his mind from the outset, or whether he became disgruntled over something and so hatched the plot, we don't know. It's true he had asked for an increase of salary, but as he was being paid at the full standard rate it had to be refused. Be that as it may, he has now shown his hand.'

'What does it look like?'

'Pretty grim. He's got us by the short hairs and he knows it. He has in his possession documents, either the originals or microfilm copies, of a nature so secret that if they were handed over to one of our enemies, or even if they were made public, they could have results which could only be described as devastating. He must have been collecting this sort of material for some time before he made his break.'

'Are these some sort of plans – blueprints, or things of that nature?'

'No. As far as we can make out Neckel has taken the originals or copies of secret correspondence between ourselves and our allies. These include references to our defence programmes which have taken years to prepare. Imagine what it would mean if every nation in the Western Alliance had to revise its entire organisation – as a result of what would be said to be carelessness on our part.'

'What does he intend to do with this dynamite?'

He's using it as a means of blackmail. He demands the sum of one million dollars for the return of the documents.'

'A million! By thunder! He must realise their value.'

'Of course he does. He would choose them for that reason. To make matters worse it now appears that while he was working for us he was carrying out experiments on his own account, the results of which he kept to himself. Just what they were we don't know; he doesn't say; but we can assume this information to be of capital importance.'

'Would the government pay a million dollars to get this stuff back?'

'Certainly. But how can we be sure of getting it? You know how blackmailers work. With the dollars in his pocket he could vanish again with the documents still in his possession, and so retain the whip hand of us. In fact, not only would we have thrown away a million dollars, but there would be nothing to prevent him from offering the documents to, say, Russia, for a similar, or even a larger sum of money.'

Biggles tapped the ash off his cigarette. 'So that's it. But he can't avoid the difficulty every blackmailer must face, which is how to collect the money without being caught.'

The Air Commodore smiled wanly. 'Don't fool yourself. He has that all very nicely planned. When he left England he went first to the United States and there opened a bank account. What we are told to do now is pay the million dollars into that account. It's as simple as that. One month later the documents will be returned to us by post. The reason for the delay of a month is plain enough to see. It would give him time to withdraw the money from the bank, convert it into any currency that might suit him, and open another account in any city in the world, possibly under another name.'

'The cunning devil.'

'We're dealing with a clever man. Neckel has a brain and knows how to use it. He seems to have thought of everything.'

'Couldn't you ask the United States government to advise the bank what's in the wind and jump the scoundrel when he calls to collect the cash?'

'He's made provision for that. He informs us that when he goes to the bank to draw the money the documents will have been parcelled and addressed to a certain Soviet embassy. Should he not return from the bank he has arranged for the parcel to be posted. Thus, as he points out, we might get his body, but in so doing we would have made a present to Russia of the documents.'

'Smart guy. What else does he say?'

'He has handed us an ultimatum. If the money has not been paid into the bank in one month he will offer the parcel to Russia, anyway. We now have just over three weeks left to comply.'

Biggles reached for another cigarette. 'So you're in touch with this sharper.'

'Yes. By correspondence.'

'Where is he?'

'He's living in a place called Cruzuado. We don't know his actual address. He collects mail under a post-office number.'

'Where is this place? I've never heard of it.'

'I'm not surprised. Again we can see how carefully he made his plan. Cruzuado is a small town, population about three thousand, in Peru, on the eastern side of the Andes at the point where Peru, Brazil and Bolivia meet. It's on the bank of one of the several rivers in the region, the Rio Jurara, one of the upper tributaries of the Rio Madeira which in turn is a tributary of the Amazon, the confluence being near Manaos, which as you know is a thousand miles from the sea.'

Biggles looked puzzled. 'What's the idea of burying himself in the back of beyond?'

The Air Commodore smiled wryly. 'The reasons aren't hard to find. In the first place he knows the country, and may have visited Cruzuado when he lived in Peru. But the place has another advantage, a strategical one. Apparently Neckel knows all about the difficulties of extradition. At Cruzuado he has three countries at his disposal, and a mere step will take him from one to the other. You don't need me to tell you the difficulties of getting an extradition warrant even when we have an agreement with the country concerned. Where no agreement exists it's practically impossible to get one.'

Biggles nodded.

'Even allowing that Peru, knowing all the circumstances, did agree to co-operate, negotiations would take months. Apart from that, too many people would have to know what was going on. At the first whisper Neckel would simply have to paddle a canoe across the river into Brazil and we would have to start all over again. If there was more trouble he could step into Bolivia. That's no use. Neckel could play cat and mouse with us for years, and we'd be powerless to do anything about it. How could the thing be kept secret in those conditions? We'd be the laughing stock of the whole world. Russia would get to hear about it and in all probability join in the chase after Neckel.'

'In which case they'd get him, since they don't hesitate to employ methods which would be frowned on here.'

'Yes. They have the advantage of us there.'

'So you're not thinking of trying to grab Neckel by force?'

'No. We don't want Neckel. If we had him he would only be an embarrassment. All we want are those documents, and we've got to get them somehow.'

'From the time you've spent telling me all this would

I be right in assuming you want me to tackle this job?'

'You would.'

'But why us? The Foreign Office has its own agents. Who had the bright idea that this was a job for the Air Police?'

'I don't know, but I've had my orders from a very high level and it isn't for me to question them. I imagine speed is the main factor involved. We've only a little over three weeks to get those papers or, if Neckel carries out his threat, they'll go to Russia.'

Biggles shrugged. 'Well, we've had some tall orders in the past, but this one is about the tops. Have you any suggestions as to how I should go about this?'

'None. I'm leaving that to you. You can have anything you need, and you can do anything you like as long as you get those papers. There's only one condition. The government must not in any circumstances be involved.'

'The trouble with this country is, we're too squeamish about the way we tackle traitors,' asserted Biggles bitingly. 'When some years ago a similar position arose with Russia, with Trotsky hiding out in Mexico, Moscow sent out an agent who made no bones about bashing Trotsky on the head with an ice axe.'

'Don't forget a Mexican court gave the agent a life sentence for his trouble. I'd hate to think of you spending the rest of your days in a South American prison.'

'Don't worry. I may end that way, but it won't be for splitting anyone's skull open with an axe.'

'Well, make what you can of it. There's a file with all the particulars you're likely to need, photos of Neckel

etcetera, so you'll recognise him if you see him. But
don't waste any time.'

'If this is all the information you can give me it
doesn't offer much of a chance,' said Biggles, lugubriously.

'We've done all we can at this end.'

'What does that mean?'

'We've arranged to put you in touch with an Englishman who lives in, or near, Cruzuado. He should be able
to give you the local gen.'

'What's he doing there?'

'He works there. His name is Peter Fotherham, better
known on the spot by the Spanish equivalent, Don
Pedro. He's a professional naturalist who went to the
country years ago and has never come home. He now
acts as a collecting and forwarding agent for two or
three London firms with interests in that part of the
world. The lines being orchids, butterflies and small
zoological specimens, for which there is always a market
with museums and private collectors. Apparently he
finds the stuff, crates it and sends it down the river to
Manaos, where it is picked up by one of the regular
steamship services which operate between that country
and this.'

'Can I go out by this service?'

'No. It would take too long. You'll have to fly out.
We've been in touch with one of Fotherham's
companies, the one that deals in orchids, and fixed up
for you, with one assistant, to go out as their represen-
tatives to learn that end of the business. It seems there's
more to it than one would imagine. Fotherham has been

advised so he'll be expecting you. No one has seen him for years, so you'd better be prepared for anything. We're told he's a queer type, but at all events you'll have a local contact and an excuse for being in Cruzuado. Aside from that we're also arranging with the appropriate offices in London for the papers you'll need – visas and so on. You'll travel of course as civilians, so for the time being you'd better forget that you're police officers, or anything to do with the British government.'

'Does this orchid concern know what we're really up to?'

'No. They may suspect you're on a government mission but they don't know any details. Fotherham knows nothing. He'll take you at your face value.'

'Fair enough. I suppose you don't know if Neckel has these documents with him?'

The Air Commodore smiled sadly. 'That's something he hasn't told us, and I wouldn't expect him to. But I imagine they won't be far away from where he's living. That's the first thing you'll have to find out.'

'What about his personal habits, assuming he has some? I'm thinking he may have altered his appearance.'

'I can't tell you much about that. As you'll see from his photograph he's a weedy, neurotic-looking type, dark, rather high cheek bones and black hair worn long except where it's getting a bit thin above the temples. He chain-smokes cigarettes which he rolls himself, using a dark, strong tobacco which, not surprisingly, has resulted in a smoker's throat, which reveals itself in a little dry cough. When he was here he wore a gold signet ring on the third finger of his left hand; but he may have discarded it by now. But you'll find these particulars in the file. Read it and let me have it back. When do you think you could be ready to start?'

'Tomorrow, if you'll have the papers ready.'

'I'll attend to that. Who will you take with you?'

Biggles thought for a moment. 'I think Lissie would be the best man for the job, which seems one in which he could play the dumb Englishman to advantage. Ginger is too susceptible to fever for a locality where there's bound to be plenty of it, and you'll need Algy here to take charge while I'm away.'

'All right. I'll leave it to you.'

'I'll see you again, sir.' Biggles picked up the file and left the room.

CHAPTER 3

CRUZUADO

BIGGLES and Bertie spent a comfortable night under mosquito nets, and the morning following their arrival at the Villa Vanda brought a cloudless sky and torrid heat. The sodden earth steamed. Every tree shed a shower of water every time its branches were moved by birds or monkeys. The air was full of sound. Hummingbirds hummed as they hung, apparently suspended by invisible wires, over flowers that had opened their petals to the sun. Insects chirped. Frogs boomed or quacked like ducks. Large birds whistled or uttered raucous cries.

Don Pedro, who had gone early to the pier to superintend the loading of a *callapo*, a large balsa raft, with crates of orchids consigned to the company's depot at Manaos, to take advantage of the fast-flowing river, had been as good as his word. Four rough-looking ponies were standing at the door ready for the final stage to Cruzuado. Three carried ordinary riding saddles and the fourth a pack saddle on which the water-proof kitbags had already been slung. With the horses was Don Pedro's yard man, a cheerful heavy-weight negro with a curiously small voice, named José, who was to act as guide and protector. The inevitable machete was thrust through a broad leather belt. He had been chosen for the job because he spoke a little English, having been with Don Pedro for some years.

As Biggles and Bertie got astride their mounts Don Pedro came up to say goodbye and offer a final word of advice. 'You shouldn't have any trouble in Cruzuado, but if you do, come back here. José will take care of you. You're sure your papers are in order?'

'They should be.'

'Then coming from Brazil the sooner you report to the *sub-prefecto, administrador,* the better. He knows me. He's not a bad chap, but like most of them he's apt to be officious with people who try to be smart with him. His name's Señor Vargas. Remember me to him and say you're friends of mine; that should see you all right.'

'We'll do that,' promised Biggles, and the party set off, José leading the way with the packhorse.

It was soon evident that Don Pedro's description of the track had been somewhat optimistic and it was easy to see why he didn't go to town more often than was necessary. It was no more than a wide path that had been hacked through the jungle. It was all ups and downs and rarely ran straight for any distance, being forced to make detours round obstacles such as giant trees. It was never far from the river, glimpses of which could occasionally be seen. The going underfoot was as treacherous as a jungle path can be, consisting of mud and rotting vegetable matter in which the horses, fortunately accustomed to it, squelched and slithered about as their hoofs stuck in the mire. From the broad ever-

green leaves of branches that met overhead water pat-
tered down as heavy rain. On both sides rose the virgin
forest, gloomy and foreboding, yet not without a curious
fascination. The heat in the leafy tunnel, for as such it
appeared, was sweltering. There was not a breath of
air.

They passed a small clearing in which, in front of a
primitive shelter, a party of Indians watched with im-
passive faces as the cavalcade went by. They were a
squalid, poverty-stricken lot, as so often is the case with
natives who are in touch with civilisation yet form no
part of it. José said they were wild rubber collectors who
sometimes brought in orchids to Don Pedro, who paid
them well for their trouble. The fools spent their money
on things that were no use to them. They were all right
when they were sober, but when they were drunk they
went mad, he concluded casually.

For the most part the journey was made in silence,
Biggles and Bertie being too occupied in keeping their
seats and trying to fend off the swarms of insects that
travelled with them and seemed determined to make a
meal off them or their mounts. Worst of all were what
José called *taranos,* large horse flies with a vicious
bite.

There was plenty of life along or around the path.
Parrots and parrakeets screamed overhead. Toucans uttered their absurd cries, like wheels in need of oil. Hum-
ming-birds of wonderful hues darted from flower to
flower. Monkeys chattered and whistled high in the
trees. From time to time the fragrance of some unseen
flowers came wafting through the stench of decaying

leaves. Often the track was bordered by ferns of fasci-
nating delicacy and size. Butterflies of incredible shapes
and colours crossed their path. On one occasion it was a
huge cloud of the iridescent blue Morphos. Columns of
umbrella ants crossed the trail, each individual carrying
a disc of leaf many times larger than itself.

Once Bertie had to duck to avoid collision with a
huge moth that came whirling along, a repulsive-look-
ing creature with mottled grey wings and a head like a
human skull from which projected a long needle-like
sting. José said it was *'la cigarra de la muete'*, which
could be translated as the death moth. Anyone stung by
it, he averred, either died or went raving mad in a few
hours.

'Do you really believe that?' queried Biggles, dubiously.

'I don't know,' answered José, frankly. 'I've never
been stung.' He roared with laughter at his little joke.
'No hay cuidado' (there's no need to worry), he assured
them.

'Jolly little fellows,' remarked Bertie.

There was a more serious incident when a small green
snake, not more than two feet long, suddenly landed on
the pack saddle and bounced to the ground. José was off
his horse in a flash and with one stroke of his machete
cut the creature in halves. It was, he said, as he re-
mounted, a *macabril*, and volunteered the information
that its habit was to sleep on a branch and jump on
anyone foolish enough to wake it up. Its bite, he asserted, was fatal, unless the person bitten could reach
water instantly. What the water had to do with it he did

not say. From his carefree manner it was clear that this sort of thing was normal jungle travel.

With their wet shirts sticking to their sweating bodies the party went on, and in due course José offered the good news that they hadn't much farther to go. Already, as Bertie remarked in a voice of disgust, they looked as if they had been on the trail for a week.

Across the river, from the top of a low hill, a few houses on the far bank could be seen. This, they knew, was Brazilian territory, they themselves being in Peru. A little higher up the river forked into two streams, and it was there, as they knew from an earlier study of the map, that the frontier marched with Bolivia.

There were no further incidents, and they entered a region of partial cultivation, notably coffee trees, showing their scarlet berries.

At first sight the town of Cruzuado looked a dreary, depressing place, and on closer inspection, far from improving, it was worse, being dirty as well as dilapidated. The main street up which they rode, having no surface, was simply mud; this was littered with rubbish, making it apparent that it was seldom if ever cleaned up. The houses on both sides were of the cheapest possible description, built of baked mud bricks, with the white-wash dirty and stained. Only the best could boast of corrugated iron roofs. The shops, which were small and without glass windows, were untidy and in general disarray.

There were quite a few people about, a good proportion being lithe, slim-waisted *llaneros*, their legs bowed from long hours in the saddle, their eyes mere slits from gazing over boundless, sun-scorched plains. They were all alike. All wore belts slung low across their hips, often with a revolver hanging from it. Some also carried a machete. Long, ugly spurs, with vicious rowels, clattered on their ankles. They wore tight trousers, indescribably filthy. Usually their shirts were patched and their sombreros battered all shapes.

Said Biggles to Bertie: 'Take a look at some real cowboys. A different proposition from what we're shown on the TV screens.'

José, who must have overheard the remark, said they were sad, lonely men, guarding their herds on the *llanos* for weeks, sometimes months at a time, without seeing another human being. Who was to blame them if, when they did come into town, they went a little mad?

He took his charges to the Hotel Comisaria, which stood in the *plaza*, the central square next door to the headquarters of the local authority, which included the Customs Office and the Police Station. He said he would take the horses round the back and wait until they had made their arrangements for accommodation. He would bring in the kitbags.

Biggles and Bertie, not exactly impressed by the exterior of the building, went in, and at a plain unvarnished reception desk, occupied by a pretty but cheeky half-caste girl, were able to book a double room, for which they had to make a deposit in advance. A sloe-eyed Indian boy took them up to it, and presently brought up the kitbags.

'I don't think I'm going to like this,' said Bertie, as they went up the ant-infested stairs.

He liked it even less when he had seen the bedroom. It was so small that two narrow beds could only just be fitted into it. There were no sheets. The blankets were far from clean and the mattresses were as hard as boards. The only piece of furniture was a wash-stand, with a cracked basin half full of brownish water. Nails driven into the walls served as pegs for clothes. Some empty beer bottles had been thrown in a corner. When Bertie asked the boy, when he brought the kitbags, about a bath, he was told there was a shower outside in the yard. He would have to provide his own soap and towel. The toilet was also outside.

'It seems we haven't struck the luxury class, old boy,' observed Bertie, wrinkling his nose in disgust.

'Remember where you are,' said Biggles.

'Don Pedro said the hotel wasn't too bad.'

'By comparative standards he was probably right.'

'Then I shudder to think what the cheap hotels are like.'

However, they both had a shower and put on dry shirts, after which they sought José. They found him in the bar, having a beer with some *llaneros*, and joined him. On hearing that they intended to stay he said he would return to the Villa Vanda, leaving the packhorse and their two ponies against the time when they would need them for their return journey. He had already spoken to the stable boy who, as he knew the horses belonged to Don Pedro, could be relied on to take care of them. Biggles gave José some money for food before he started for home.

They met, and made themselves known to the *patron*

of the hotel, a Mexican who was obviously proud of his establishment. 'You won't find any snakes or scorpions here,' he boasted, as he showed them the way to the dining room, which turned out to be in keeping with the rest of the place. Oddly enough, or perhaps it was because plenty of beef was available, they were served with a steak which they agreed was as good as they had ever had anywhere. Boiled rice had to serve for potatoes, which were not to be had. The fact that they were hungry may have had something to do with their appreciation of the meal.

Over a cup of locally grown coffee, which also was excellent, Bertie requested to be told the plan of campaign, if Biggles had made one.

'The first thing is to report to the *comisaria* to get our papers stamped,' answered Biggles. 'After that we shall have to try to locate the man we've come to find.'

'And how are you going to do that?'

'It would be unwise to ask questions, because word that inquiries were being made about him would be almost certain to get back to Neckel – that is, if he's still here. We're not even sure of that. All we can do for the moment is keep our eyes and ears open. We may see him, or hear a chance remark about him. I'm a bit worried about that Russian new arrival Don Pedro mentioned. It might be coincidence. On the other hand he may be here on the same job as we are. If this is the best hotel in the town he may be staying here, in which case we should be able to spot him. That's enough to go on with. Let's take a walk round the town to get our bearings. While we're at it we can present ourselves to

the *sub-prefecto,* Señor Vargas, who I imagine is boss
of the local authority. The fact that he's a pal of Don
Pedro should make things easy. That's where a local
contact comes in useful.'

'We haven't yet signed the hotel visitor's book,' reminded Bertie.

'I doubt if they bother with that sort of thing here,'
returned Biggles, a prediction that turned out to be correct, as the girl at the reception desk informed them with
a flashing smile.

'I say, you know old boy, that saucy minx has got her
eye on you,' observed Bertie.

'What she's got her eye on is a nice fat tip when we
leave,' answered Biggles cynically.

Leaving the hotel they walked the few yards to the
local government offices where, on being shown into his
office, they found Señor Vargas in conversation with a
stout, heavily moustached man, in uniform, who was
introduced to them as the *Intendente,* head of the local
military police. A half empty bottle of wine and two
glasses stood on the table between them.

The visitors were received with the courtesy that is
natural to Spaniards, or people of Spanish descent,
everywhere – provided they are not rubbed the wrong
way – and on being informed that Biggles and his friend
were British, and friends of Don Pedro at the Villa
Vanda whom they had come to see, formalities were
waived and their papers were stamped with hardly a
question asked. In fact, Señor Vargas apologised for
having to make the regular inquiry, had they anything
dutiable to declare?

Biggles listed the few articles they had brought with them, paid the small Customs due requested, and that was that.

Knowing that inevitably there would be some curiosity as to their purpose in being in Cruzuado, Biggles offered the information that they had come from England to see Don Pedro on a matter of business, chiefly connected with orchids, and were hoping to stay a little while to see something of the country.

'As you will have noticed, it is very beautiful, and the accommodation is excellent,' declared Señor Vargas cheerfully.

He obviously believed this, and Biggles thought it prudent to agree. Anyway, he had no complaints, realising the difficulties of keeping law and order in a vast area, most of it untamed, far removed from the capital. Moreover, he liked the man who, although far from having an imposing figure, being small and lean, looked tough, and well able to hold down his job.

After that they were all good friends together, their respective nations being toasted in a glass of wine. The Chief of Police assured them that they could rely on him always being at their service.

After they had left the office Biggles said he had been tempted to ask, casually, if there was a man Neckel living in the town, but had decided it was too early to ask such a personal question. That might come at their next meeting. He did go so far as to ask if there were any other British visitors in the town – supposing that Neckel would be traveling on his British passport – but on receiving an answer in the negative did not pursue the matter.

'It looks as if Neckel may be passing himself off as a Peruvian, which of course he could, quite easily, having been brought up in Peru,' he told Bertie.

They took a walk round the town, waiting outside the post-office for a while in the hope that they might catch sight of Neckel; but to no purpose. They also looked in some of the bars, and had coffee at a café, with the same object in view, but saw no one remotely resembling the man they sought.

Finally, feeling they had done enough for one day, they returned to their hotel for the night.

'One thing we can be sure of is this,' said Biggles, speaking quietly, for the walls were mere matchboarding. 'If Neckel is only half as clever as we've been given to believe, he'll anticipate the move our people have made, I mean, he'll be prepared for agents to be sent out to locate him. It follows, therefore, that he'll be on the watch for any new arrivals, whatever nationality they may be, or pretend to be. I'm afraid he's more likely to spot us than we are to see him.'

CHAPTER 4

THE BAR FRANCISCO

BIGGLES was beginning to get worried.

Three days had passed, and in spite of all their efforts they had achieved nothing. Not that there was very much they could do. They had watched the post-office for long periods hoping to catch sight of their man; they had wandered round the public places, the bars, the cafés and even the cinema; they had listened to conversations; they had hung about the food shops to observe the customers; but all to no purpose.

What Biggles did not like was the behaviour of the Russian, of whom Don Pedro had spoken and who was staying at their hotel. He seemed to be doing the same thing as themselves, wandering about the town with apparently no particular object in view. Was he watching them, or was he, too, looking for the runaway scientist? They didn't know. They knew him well by sight, chiefly from seeing him in the dining room, but had not spoken to him, having no reasonable excuse for doing so. Aside from that, all they knew about him was his surname, Bogosoff, from having heard it spoken by the *patron*, and the fact that he spoke Spanish fluently.

As Biggles had said at the outset, the trouble, or difficulty, of the situation was that they dare not ask questions, not only because word of such inquiries might get back to Neckel but for fear people would suspect they had an ulterior motive for being in the town; bearing in mind that according to Don Pedro quite a few of them were refugees from the law in their own countries. They would therefore be suspicious on their own account of people who asked questions.

They had kept an eye on their horses to see they were properly fed and watered by the Indian stable lad in charge.

The weekend had passed off without any serious trouble although there had been some drunken behaviour, including fights, which as far as they know had not gone beyond wrestling and fisticuffs. As Don Pedro had warned them would happen, a fair number of *llaneros,* easily recognisable by their clothes, had ridden in, most of them leaving their horses at the hitching rails provided for that purpose in the square.

A disturbing factor that could not be overlooked was the possibility that Neckel was not there at all. He might be residing in another town. He might even have crossed the river into Brazil, or moved into Boliva, no great distance away. In that case, as Biggles pointed out to Bertie, they were wasting their time.

'But what about his letters? Surely he'd come in for them?' queried Bertie.

'He might send somebody for them.'

'True enough.'

'If we don't soon get a lead we shall have to ask questions, regardless of the consequences.'

'Where would you do that?'

'The most obvious place is the post-office. We could ask if Neckel is still calling there for his letters.'

'He may be using another name, in which case the answer would be no.'

'That's another snag. Failing the post-office I'd try Señor Vargas. He should know something about strangers who come and go. Better still, we could go back to Don Pedro, and putting our cards on the table ask him to help us. After all, he's British. Being as well known as he is, he could get away with questions more easily than we would, having only just arrived. He must know a good many people here, the shopkeepers where he gets his stores, for instance. Dash it all, if Neckel is here he must either buy his food or eat out somewhere.'

'As you said about the letters, if he's the crafty customer we're told he is he could get a servant to do that for him.'

Biggles nodded. 'I realise that. Well, it's no use going on like this; we're running out of time. Tomorrow I shall go to the post-office.'

In the event it did not come to that, for shortly after this conversation they got, in a curious fashion, if not a clue, a piece of information that might lead to one.

It happened like this. On returning to the hotel for lunch who did they find in the hall, apparently flirting with the half-caste girl at the reception counter, but José.

'Hello! What are you doing here?' asked Biggles.

'Don Pedro sent me in to see if you and the horses are all right, *señor*.'

'Come and have a drink. This is a thirsty climate.'

At the bar Biggles continued, in a bantering voice: 'José, I'm beginning to think you're a sly old dog. What were you saying to that saucy young woman in the hall when we came in?'

José, affected innocence. 'Me, *señor*? I don' say nothin'. She speaks to me. Yes, I'll have a beer, please, *señor*.'

'And what had she to say?'

'She asks me about you.'

Biggles' expression changed. 'Is that so? What did she want to know?'

'Where you come from, how long you stay and what you do here.'

'What did you tell her?'

'I say you are friends of Don Pedro, come to see him.'

'Why is she interested in us?'

'She says a *señor* gives her some money to tell him of any new *gringos* who arrive at the hotel.'

Biggles caught Bertie's eye. 'Indeed. Who is this inquisitive *señor*?'

'She don' say?'

'Where does he live?'

'She says she don' know.'

'Then how does she give the information to him? Does he come here for it?'

'No, *señor*. She meets him outside after she finish here. He buys her many drinks.'

'Where do they meet?'

'She don' say.'

'Have you any idea why this man should be interested in *gringos* who come to the hotel?'

José grinned broadly. 'Maybe he has a gold-mine to sell. One of them smart guys, perhaps, who live by selling gold-mines and maps to show where old treasures are hid.'

'You talk as if that was quite a business here.'

'Yes, sah. Good business. All new men who come here want a gold-mine, and plenty of men here to sell one.' José laughed.

Biggles thought for a moment. 'It could be I'd like to buy a gold-mine myself.'

José looked surprised. 'You don't go for dat bunkum, *señor*. No good. If a man has a gold-mine he keep it.'

'You're a wise man, José. But I'd like to see the man who asks questions about us. You know this girl pretty well, I fancy?'

'Pretty good. Know her long time.'

'Then I want you to find out from her the name of this man who is interested in *gringos*, and where she meets him.'

José looked doubtful. 'May be she don' talk. Say she forget.'

'Does she like money?'

'Plenty.'

'Then give her this, and see if it will help her to remember.' Biggles peeled some notes from his wad. 'Be careful how you go about it. We'll wait here.'

'*Si, señor*.' José finished his beer and strolled away.

'This is better,' said Biggles, softly, to Bertie. 'Now we may get somewhere.'

It was a little while before José came back.

'Well?' inquired Biggles, a trifle anxiously.

José cast a furtive glance around. 'Better not talk here,' he said. 'Outside, in the yard.'

'What did you find out?' asked Biggles, when they were in the shade of the stables.

'That gal Dolores she scared to talk too much,' answered José. 'She says she meets man every night in the Bar Francisco. He buys her plenty drinks.'

'What time?'

'Eleven o'clock.'

'What's his name?'

'Luis Salvador.'

'Where does he live?'

'Dolores say she don' know that. When he first comes here he stays in hotel for three days. Then he goes. Dolores think not far away.'

'What country does this man Salvador come from?'

'She not know that.'

'She told him about us?'

'She tells him about all *gringos* who come.'

'Anything else?'

'One other thing, *señor*. When she meets him she take any letters for him at post-office.'

'Does she though! Good work, José. You've done well. How long are you staying in the town?'

'I go back now to Villa Vanda.'

'All right. You can tell Don Pedro that all is well with us and we hope to see him shortly.'

'*Si Señor.*' José went over to his horse, which he had left at a hitching rail, and went off.

'What do you make of all this?' Bertie asked Biggles.

'It's too early to come to any conclusion; but with any luck we should be able to get a glimpse tonight of this man who calls himself Salvador. That may be his real name. Of course, his purpose in wanting to know about all foreigners arriving at the hotel may have nothing whatever to do with us. It's unlikely that Neckel is the only man here who has reason to be suspicious of visitors. One thing is clear. This fellow Salvador has something to hide or he wouldn't be behaving as he is.'

'What about this girl Dolores?'

'She doesn't come into it. She's merely a tool, a spy. I wouldn't trust her a yard, anyway. She'd sell anybody for money. All the same, I'd say she told José the truth, as far as she knows it.'

'What are you going to do – go to this Bar Francisco and watch what happens?'

'Of course. I want to see this man Salvador. It could be Neckel, or a man employed by him. Neckel, having been born in the country, would have no difficulty in passing himself off as a local. But I can't very well go to the bar, late at night, dressed like this. Among the sort of people who I imagine use the place I'd feel a bit conspicuous.'

'What will you do about it?'

'As you know, I'm not much for disguises, but I shall

have to get some different togs – make myself look more as if I belonged to the place. It shouldn't be difficult. All I aim to do is watch without being noticed.'

'Do you want me to come with you?'

'I'll think about that and decide later. When we've had something to eat we'll get the outfits. I've noticed two or three shops where they sell clothes.'

They went back into the hotel where, in the bar, they saw Bogosoff in earnest conversation with a dark-skinned type who looked like a native. He was a seedy-looking individual with two front teeth missing. He wore a bush jacket that had once been white, and an old pith helmet of the same colour.

'So our Russian friend has found a pal,' murmured Biggles, as they went through to the dining room.

The rest of the day passed quietly. All they had to do was provide themselves with the kit they needed, not as a disguise but merely to make themselves less noticeable among the sort of clientele that might be expected to patronise the Bar Francisco. This became more de-sirable when they had had a look at the place from the outside. It was larger than Biggles expected, but it was a drab, slovenly-looking establishment; in fact, nothing more than a low dive, typical of several they had seen.

Biggles regarded the place critically as they walked past. 'I don't know how the town goes for common thugs and pick-pockets, but in that sort of den anything could happen,' he observed. 'We shall have to take some money with us, but I'm not taking into that hole any-thing I'd be sorry to lose. We'd better leave our identification papers in our room. I don't suppose the hotel possesses a safe, and I wouldn't trust it if it did, so we shall have to find somewhere to hide them.'

Returning to the hotel they had their evening meal, after which, in their room, they tried on their newly acquired garments. At the finish Biggles might have passed for a fairly prosperous trader. Bertie was content with a shirt in the common local style, a plaited straw sombrero and, for good measure, a machete hanging from his belt. This was merely a whimsey, an ornament that amused him. He hoped he would never have to use it.

'Better leave that eyeglass of yours at home,' advised Biggles. 'It might cause a riot.'

It was about a quarter to eleven when they set off for the rendezvous, not more than a quarter of a mile away.

Biggles had decided that they might as well both go in, but not together, although inside they would keep close enough to be in touch by word or signal.

Now that darkness had fallen, the kind of place they purposed entering was made evident before they reached it, when to their ears came the strumming of a string instrument and a babble of many voices. As they approached the door two *llaneros* staggered out locked in a tight embrace. Breaking apart, one knocked down the other, whereupon the man who had fallen got to his feet, and producing a bottle from somewhere hurled it at his opponent. It struck the wall and shattered. The thrower strode away, muttering. The other went back into the tavern.

'Very pretty,' said Bertie, brightly.

In accordance with the plan Biggles went in first, leaving Bertie to follow in a minute or two. He was greeted by a blast of hot air in which were mingled the aromas of beer, sweat, tobacco and paraffin-burning lamps. The noise was considerable as people tried to make themselves heard above an accordion and a guitar. In a space that had been cleared at the far end of the room, a girl, crudely painted, heavily built, but attractive in a coarse sort of way, was whirling her skirts in a Spanish dance. She wore huge earrings. Bracelets jangled on her wrists. For the rest, there might have been a score of customers, chiefly *llaneros*. Most of them lounged against a bar where drinks were being served by a man and a woman, swarthy, black-haired and dark-eyed. A few other people were seated in twos and threes at small bamboo tables laden with beer bottles and glasses. At one table four men were playing cards. Only one man was sitting alone.

Biggles collected a glass of beer from the bar, and finding a vacant table in the background sat down to survey the scene.

A minute later Bertie entered and did the same thing, choosing a table adjacent to the one occupied by Biggles, now trying to pick out the man they had come to inspect, if he was already there.

Naturally, his eyes dwelt on the man who sat alone. He was slumped in his chair, and appeared to have had plenty to drink, if he wasn't actually drunk. Could this be Salvador – or the man who was calling himself by that name? From what could be seen of his face under a wide-brimmed hat he certainly didn't look like Neckel,

thought Biggles. He seemed to be about the right build,
but he wore a beard, untrimmed, and did not look very
clean. Watching him closely he thought again when the
man took out a tobacco pouch and rolled a cigarette.
But this, as he soon realised, was nothing to go by, because most of the *llaneros* rolled their own cigarettes.
From time to time the man he was watching coughed,
a little hard cough, but that, in such an atmosphere,
was understandable. Biggles had also found himself
coughing as the pungent reek of raw tobacco bit into his
nose and throat. He remembered the signet ring which
Neckel had been in the habit of wearing and his eyes
switched to the man's hands. He wore no ring. But that
again proved nothing, as he might have stopped wearing
it or perhaps had taken it off rather than let it be seen in
the bar.

The situation remained unchanged for some minutes.
The girl finished her dance to a burst of applause, and
there were shouts of '*bravo, Maria,*' evidently her name,
as she mingled with the customers. A man handed her a
drink, whereupon she walked over to Bertie and sat on
his lap. This was probably intended to be no more than
a harmless joke; but Bertie, taken by surprise, apparently didn't see it like that. Foolishly perhaps, he pushed
her off, whereupon she slapped his face and spat on the
floor. This brought shouts of ribald laughter.

Biggles didn't laugh. He didn't like this at all. Bertie
had become conspicuous and he could see the makings
of a first-class row. For a minute he feared they were
going to be involved in a rough house, for the girl was
obviously popular. But to his relief the man behind the

counter shouted something and Maria rejoined the men at the bar.

Then into the room came Dolores, the girl from their hotel, now over-smartly dressed and scarlet lipped but really quite pretty in an exotic sort of way. Biggles pulled down the brim of his hat as she passed close to him on her way to the man he had been watching. She joined him at his table. He rose unsteadily and fetched two drinks from the bar.

Biggles saw he had been right in supposing the man to be Salvador.

As the pair settled down and started talking with their heads close together, into the saloon walked Bogosoff and the man with whom he had been seen in the hotel. They took up positions at a table as far away as possible from the noisy crowd at the bar.

This was a development Biggles did not expect and he did some quick thinking. Had they come into the place merely by chance or had he and Bertie been followed? Or was it Dolores who had been followed? There was no indication.

For some minutes Dolores and Salvador sat talking. Then, suddenly, they got up and walked towards the door.

'Follow them to see where they go,' said Biggles tersely to Bertie. 'See you later at the hotel.'

Dolores and Salvador went out with Bertie close behind them.

Almost on their heels went Bogosoff and his companion, much to Biggles' chagrin, for his object in sending Bertie to follow Salvador was that he might stay and watch Bogosoff. There was little time for thought, and as there was now no point in staying on alone he made up his mind quickly to follow. But again his purpose was defeated, for at that moment a fight broke out and it was a minute or two before he could get to the door. By the time he was out on the road the others had disappeared. Moreover, there was no one near to tell him which way they had gone.

The moon was not yet up, and he realised that to look for them in the dark would be an almost hopeless proposition; so, after a brief hesitation, feeling frustrated he made his way slowly to the hotel.

The time was after midnight when he walked in, but confident that Bertie would not be long he decided to wait in the bar. In this, however, he was mistaken. Time dawdled on. One o'clock came and there was still no sign of Bertie. It was then he had his first twinge of uneasiness. But there was nothing he could do. When the hands of the clock had crawled round to two o'clock, with still no Bertie, he became really worried; but perceiving it would be futile to go out hoping to find him all he could do was go up to his room.

CHAPTER 5

THE HOUSE
IN THE FOREST

IT was with no thought of danger in his mind that Bertie left the Bar Francisco to follow Dolores, or, more particularly, her male companion.

He, no more than Biggles, knew for certain who the man was: there had been no opportunity to discuss what they had seen in the bar: the only thing not in doubt was, this was the man who, according to what the half-caste girl had told José, had so much interest in newly arrived foreigners. She had given his name as Salvador, so it was reasonable to assume that the man in front was the one known by that name.

It did not follow that he was Neckel, hiding his face behind a beard and his identity under a false name. But there was a chance that it might be. Or he might be a man employed by him to undertake his errands. Against that it might well turn out to be that he was a man whose interest in *gringos* had nothing whatever to do with the reason that had brought them to the country. What they were doing, therefore, was really a shot in the dark in the hope of it finding the absconding scientist, for until they knew where he had hidden himself – always assuming he was still there – they were helpless to proceed with the object of their mission.

It was a heavy, sultry, tropical night, with the stars hanging like jewels from a ceiling of dark purple velvet, giving ample light for Bertie's purpose. A pallid glow, showing above the inky silhouette of the forest which everywhere pressed close to the town, revealed that the moon was on its way to join the stars and so make the task easier.

He took the usual precautions to prevent what he was doing from being realised by the couple he was shadowing. As his job was simply to discover their destination, which he imagined would be Salvador's residence, he went no closer than was necessary to keep them in sight. With few people about, and none when they had reached the end of the main street, this appeared to offer no difficulty.

With his eyes always on his quarry he walked on at the pace set by it, neither advancing nor dropping back. That he himself might be followed, or that someone else might be engaged in the same operation, was a thought that never occurred to him. Not once did he stop, and not once did he look round. So he was unaware that a shadowing figure was also keeping time not far behind him. It is unlikely that he would have paid any attention even if he had noticed it, because there had been no indication of such a possibility.

The houses ended, giving way to some small trees standing in rows, evidently a plantation. What the trees were he neither knew nor cared, but he was worried by the shadows they threw across the road, making visibility ahead confusing. The mosquitoes were troublesome, but that was to be expected. Occasionally he caught a glimpse of the river on his left, although he was a fair distance above it.

When something like nearly half a mile had been covered in this manner he began to wonder how much farther they were going. The road, which had deteriorated to a track, now split, the wider part wandering on into the forest, and a secondary track, little more than a wide footpath, diving down steeply towards the river. For a moment, at the junction, he was at fault, uncertain which way the couple had gone. He could no longer see them, but listening he could hear them, and went on down the narrow path guided by the sound of their voices.

The path did not go far. In a minute or two he caught a gleam of white through the trees as the moon, now above the horizon, threw a beam on the upper part of a building. This suggested he had reached the end of the trail, and so it proved. Somewhere in front a gate creaked. The sound of footsteps died away.

He went on, slowly, surveying the scene ahead, concentrating his attention of course on the house. Through some shrubs covered with large waxen blossoms he made it out to be a white-painted bungalow of some size, in better condition than the general run of houses in the district. Trees crowded down to it on three sides, but the front was clear and ran down in a shallow slope to the river. It ended at a small piece of wharfing, obviously intended to provide a mooring for a canoe that lay alongside. The only sound was the rippling of the fast running water, silver in the moonlight. He could see no one. Fireflies danced between the trees.

He stood still to consider the situation. He was not very happy about it, for if Salvador and Dolores were as thick as they appeared to be it seemed certain that the girl would tell the man that two *gringos* were interested in his movements. Or would she? To do that would mean that she had been talking. Knowing where the money José had given her had come from she was hardly likely to mention that, anyway. It seemed that Biggles hadn't been far wrong when he said he wouldn't trust the girl a yard. It seemed probable that her services were for sale to the highest bidder.

Advancing cautiously to the garden gate he soon found what he hoped to find; the name of the house. On a plain piece of board, nailed to one of the white plaster pillars that supported the gate, was painted, in bold letters *Casa Floresta*. Under it was a secondary notice that looked more recent: *Se Prohibe la Entrada,* which Bertie correctly translated as 'No admittance.'

A light appeared in the trees beside the house. With it came the soft murmur of voices. Thinking he might as well see all there was to see while he was there, Bertie moved his position to one that gave him a clearer view of the light, and the speakers. He found himself looking into a small courtyard, enclosed by flowers and flowering shrubs, with a direct entrance to the house, the door of which stood open. Standing about was some attractive garden furniture, including a table, a long seat and some chairs. A lighted lamp stood on the table. Towards the seat two people were making their way. They were Salvador and Dolores, the man carrying a bottle of wine, already uncorked, and two glasses. He stood the glasses on the table and poured some wine into them. They then sat together on the seat. With moths fluttering around the lamp and fireflies waltzing non-stop in the background it all made a quite enchanting picture.

But Bertie was not interested in pictures at that moment. He was more concerned to see, or hear, what this meeting was about. He knew only a little Spanish but he hoped it would be enough to give him the gist of the conversation, particularly if names were mentioned. He moved a little nearer. But Salvador and Dolores were talking softly, their heads together in the manner of conspirators, and he could not catch a word.

He had just decided he had done enough, for his chief purpose was to learn the name of the house, and he was about to retire when in a matter of seconds the scene changed. The garden gate was flung open, and into the courtyard bounced another woman. It was her figure rather than her face that told Bertie who she was. She was the girl Maria, who had been doing the Spanish dance in the Bar Francisco; and it was instantly clear from the torrent of words that poured from her lips that she was in a flaming temper.

Dolores, who had sprung to her feet the moment Maria made her dramatic entrance, looked for a moment as if she was going to bolt; and she may have done that had not Salvador held her back.

Maria strode up to him and pointing an accusing finger let fly a stream of words. This was loud enough for Bertie to hear, but too fast and furious for him to follow. What developed was obviously a passionate

quarrel, in which the chief speakers were Salvador and
Maria. Dolores shrank back looking scared. Actions
made it clear what the fuss was about. It was the old
story of jealousy. Two women and one man. Maria
would not stop, her voice sometimes rising to a shout.
Salvador did his best to pacify her with a glass of wine,
but far from accepting it she knocked it out of his hand.
The glass crashed.

All this meant nothing to Bertie, who watched Salvador's discomfiture with amusement until the storm
blew itself out, Maria desisting from breathlessness.
After the tempest came the lull, and in the pause Maria
seemed to remember something. She said something to
Salvador in a low voice at the same time pointing
towards the path. The only words Bertie caught were
'Bar Francisco', and they conveyed nothing. But apparently they meant something to Salvador, who walked
quickly into the house.

Deciding he had seen and heard enough, and was
unlikely to learn more, Bertie backed quietly out of the
bushes, and on reaching the path started on his way
home.

He reached the fork, and there paused for a minute
peering up the wider track, hoping to see some indication of its purpose. He was just moving on when a
sudden sound behind caused him to spin round. He
caught a split-second glimpse of a shadowy figure standing close with an arm raised; then something seemed to
explode in his head in a blaze of white light, which,
spinning faster and faster, turned to orange, from orange
to crimson, and finally to black.

CHAPTER 6

BIGGLES HAS A FRIGHT

It was about five in the morning when Biggles, tired of waiting for Bertie, sound asleep in bed, was awakened by a hammering on the door of his room, although he had left it unlocked for Bertie to get in. Still half asleep and wondering what the noise was about he scrambled out of bed, and having lit the candle, called 'Come in'.

The door was thrown open and into the room came the *Intendente*, a uniform jacket over pyjamas. Close behind came the *patron* of the hotel, in a night-shirt, wide-eyed, hair tousled, obviously just roused from his bed.

'What is it?' demanded Biggles, staring at his visitors in astonishment.

The police officer answered. 'Your friend, *señor*.'

'What about him?'

The officer shrugged. 'He must have been very drunk last night.'

'Drunk!' exclaimed Biggles. 'Nonsense. He never gets drunk.'

'He has a fall and hurts his head.'

'He didn't fall because he was drunk, I can assure you of that,' retorted Biggles. A thought struck him. 'Are you trying to tell me he's dead?'

'Not dead, *señor*, but very sick. Also he has been robbed. His pockets are empty.'

'Where is he?'

'In the police bureau. We have a room for people who get hurt. It happens many times.'

'How did he get there?'

'He was found by a young woman. She thinks he is dead. She tells one of my *agentes* who, with the help of a passing *llanero*, carried him in. I send for the doctor who says he is not dead. Then I come to tell you.'

'Where was he found?'

'In the street.'

'Where in the street?'

'At the far end of the main street. We thought you should be told of this.'

'Quite right, *señor*. I'm much obliged to you. Please take me to him.'

'*Si, señor.*'

Pulling on his shoes and slipping on a jacket, Biggles followed the two men down to the hall, where the *patron* left them, saying he would make coffee.

In a minute or two Biggles was being shown into a small stuffy room where, on a mattress not too clean, Bertie was sitting up. His face was ashen; there was a bandage over the top of his head; his face and arms were covered with hundreds of minute spots of blood where mosquitoes had been busy on him, presumably while he lay unconscious before being found. His eyes were open, but he looked dazed, and could only smile weakly, in recognition, when Biggles walked in.

'Sorry, old boy,' he breathed, his lips just moving.

On the cinema screen, from the way men recover from a blow on the head in a matter of seconds, and then resume a fight, or whatever they were doing, as if nothing had happened, it might be supposed that to be knocked unconscious by a heavy instrument is a trivial affair. In actual fact it is nothing of the sort. How long it takes the victim to recover depends of course on the force of the blow, where it strikes, and any protection the person struck may have on his head at the time. Which explains why policemen were, and sometimes still are, issued with helmets. But as a general rule, if a person has been really knocked out by a deliberate crack on the skull it is some time before he fully recovers consciousness.

At the time he was struck Bertie was wearing a sombrero, and being fortunate in having a thick crop of hair, these together may have absorbed enough of the shock to prevent his skull from being fractured. But they did not save him from slight concussion, wherefore he still looked groggy and was obviously in no state to do anything. It was evident from the number of mosquito bites that he must have lain unconscious for a long time before he was picked up. And it is not surprising that at first he was thought to be dead.

Biggles went over and knelt beside him. 'All right. Take it easy,' he said. 'Don't try to talk now.' Turning to the police officer he went on: 'I think he'd be more comfortable in his own bed, where I can look after him. Could you get someone to help me to get him there?'

'*Sin duda, señor*. It would be better so. We haven't much room here.'

'Did the doctor put that bandage on his head?'

'Yes.'

'Did he say anything about coming back?'

'No. He said he could do no more.'

'Then there's no damage apart from his head?'

'No.'

'By the way, who was the young woman who found him? I must thank her.'

'The girl they call Dolores.'

Biggles's eyebrows went up. 'You mean the girl who works at the desk in the hotel?'

'The same. Excuse me.'

The *Intendente* went off, presently to return with two of his staff who apparently he had fetched from their sleeping quarters. Between them all they got Bertie to his bed in the hotel, where his clothes were taken off and his pyjamas put on. Actually, he was able to walk, but he was still unsteady on his legs and needed support. This was watched by the *patron*, who reappeared with the pot of coffee he had promised. He did not stay.

Having seen Bertie comfortable, the police officer was about to go when he turned and eyed Biggles shrewdly. 'I will find the man who did this,' he said. 'Tell me, *señor*. Were you expecting this attack?'

'Certainly not.'

'Are you sure you have not made an enemy since you came to our country?'

Biggles hesitated as an idea struck him. He took a chance. 'There was a little trouble with a man named Neckel. Do you know him?'

The *Intendente* thought for a moment. 'No. I cannot recall that name.'

'You would have known of him had he come here?'

'But yes. He must come to me for his papers to be stamped.'

'Then it couldn't have been him,' said Biggles casually, brushing the matter aside as of no consequence.

Saying he would look in again later, when Señor Lissie was well enough to make a statement, the Chief of Police departed.

Left alone with Bertie, Biggles sponged the blood spots of the mosquito bites from his face and arms and gave him some coffee. 'Don't try to talk until you feel like it,' he said.

'I'm feeling better every minute,' declared Bertie.

'Try to get some sleep.'

'I couldn't. My head's opening and shutting. Someone certainly fetched me a real wallop on the boko.'

'Now tell me, who did it?'

'I haven't the remotest idea.'

Biggles looked taken aback. 'You really mean – you haven't even a suspicion?'

'Not a bally inkling.'

'Hadn't you noticed anybody in the street?'

'Street? I wasn't in the street, or near it.'

'You were found in the street.'

'The deuce I was! Then somebody must have dumped me there.'

'Where were you, then, when you were coshed?'

'Getting on for a mile beyond the end of the street; not

far from Salvador's house, and that's outside the town.'

'So you got as far as that.'

'Yes. I was watching the house for a while. I was on my way home when someone came up behind me. With trees on both sides it was dark. I heard a sound and looked round just too late. I caught the merest glimpse of a shadowy figure, and *wham*. All I can say is, it was a man.'

'When you're well enough you can tell me all about it.'

'I can tell you now.'

'Sure you feel up to it?'

'Absolutely. The coffee has worked wonders. The mosquitoes didn't half have a go at me. Do I itch!'

'You must have been out for a long time. You weren't found until about an hour ago. What time do you reckon it was when you took the knock?'

'It couldn't have been much after twelve.'

Biggles pulled a face. 'As long as that!'

'I'd better tell you the whole story; then you see what you can make of it.'

'Go ahead. Take your time. Don't overdo it.'

Thereupon Bertie described in detail everything that happened from the time he left the Bar Francisco to the moment he was struck. 'One thing I can tell you is this. In the Bar I got the impression that Salvador was drunk.'

'So did I.'

'He wasn't. That was an act he put on. As soon as he

was outside he walked as straight as a guardsman on parade.'

'Biggles shook his head. 'What a mix-up. This'll take some sorting out. Bogosoff and his pal followed you out of the Bar – or maybe they were tailing Salvador. I don't know. Did you see anything of them?'

'No.'

'Did you see anybody?'

'Not a soul except the party at Salvador's house.'

'You know who found you?'

'No.'

'Dolores.'

'You don't say! How could that happen?'

'She must have been on her way home. She could have had nothing to do with the coshing or she wouldn't have reported it. She certainly couldn't have carried you to where you were found – anyway, not without help.'

Bertie agreed.

'It looks as if three people were behind you when you tailed Salvador to his house. Bogosoff and his pal and that dancer, Maria, who turned up after you were there.'

'But why should any of them go for me?'

'Bogosoff may have had a reason. They say he's a Russian. He could be a spy. He might be here on the same job as ourselves, and has realised why we're here. Russia may know about Neckel absconding. Neckel may have been in touch with them. It's no use saying how could Russia know Neckel was here. How *do* spies find these things out? If it comes to that, we still don't know if Neckel is here. We think he may be Salvador.

But we only think. We don't know. We may be barking up the wrong tree. I'd like to see him in daylight.'

'Where does Maria come in?'

Biggles shrugged. 'Search me. But it rather looks as if Salvador has been amusing himself with two women with the inevitable result that now they've got wise to it the balloon has gone up. You say that in the middle of the row Maria said something to Salvador which caused him to go into the house?'

'That's how it looked to me.'

'I wonder if she spotted you before she joined the others? Is that what she told Salvador? If so he may have gone into the house to send a manservant out to find the prowler, and deal with him. Mind you, we mustn't lose sight of the possibility that this was an ordinary robbery, nothing to do with why we are here. You know your pockets are empty?'

'No. I didn't know that.'

'That may mean nothing. It could be your money was pinched to make the thing look like common thuggery.'

'What I don't understand is, if the intention was to bump me off, why didn't they throw me in the river? Why go to the trouble of lugging me all the way to the town?'

'You make a point there. They may have thought you were dead. The *Intendente* told me he thought you were a gonner when you were brought in. Salvador wouldn't want a corpse lying near his premises. Had he, or whoever was responsible, thrown you in the river, you would have been reported missing. That would have resulted in the police paying a visit to Salvador, because I would have told them you'd left the Bar Francisco to follow him. Salvador, whoever he may be, wouldn't want the police at his house asking awkward questions. I wonder how much Dolores knows. She may know what he's doing here. This isn't a tourist resort, so he must have a definite object in being here.'

'People could say that of us.'

'No. Provision was made for that by bringing in Don Pedro. We're here to do business with him in orchids, and he'd confirm that if he was questioned.'

'Why don't you have a word with Dolores?'

Biggles looked dubious. 'I doubt if she'd tell me anything even if she knows something. She'd be more likely to let something drop if she was chatting with José. Pity he isn't here. It might be worth while sending a message to him asking him to come in. Another thing I might do when it gets light is have a look at the spot where you were coshed. There might be a clue there as to who did it. It could do no harm to have a dekko, anyway. Where exactly did it happen?'

'The last thing I remember I was standing at the place where the road forks, as I told you it did. I was just turning away from the broad track to walk back to the town. You can't miss the place.'

'Was the ground soft?'

'Very.'

'Then there should be footprints.'

'There's likely to be too many. I fancy the track is well used.'

'I'll have a look at it,' decided Biggles. 'Also, I'll send

a note to Don Pedro telling him we're having a spot of
bother so could he let José come in. You try to get some
sleep. I shan't be away longer than is necessary.'

'Okay, old boy.' Bertie closed his eyes.

While he was waiting for daylight Biggles sat on his
bed and devoted his thoughts to the problem con-
fronting them. The first question was, who had struck
down Bertie, and why? Ruling out plain robbery by a
common thief – for he felt that the fact of Bertie's
pockets being emptied could be ignored – the possibilities pointed to Salvador or Bogosoff, or men employed by them. The two women in the case were hardly
worth considering. Their interests lay entirely in themselves, and however much they wanted money they were
hardly likely to resort to brute force. Neither would
carry a heavy weapon, anyway. If they used a weapon it
would be a knife or a stiletto.

Dolores was doing certain work for Salvador, so she
had a reason for being at his house. With Maria it was
different. It looked as if Salvador had been carrying on
with her. She had become suspicious of Dolores and had
simply played the part of a jealous woman by following
the couple to the Casa Floresta. She could have nothing
against Bertie sufficient to warrant an attack. Coming
face to face with Dolores she would naturally fly into a
temper.

There was no indication of where Bogosoff had gone
when he had left the Bar Francisco. It was only surmise
that he had followed anyone. It was true Biggles hadn't
seen him come in while he was waiting for Bertie. In
that case where had he gone?

Biggles concluded that the man most likely to have been responsible for the attack was Salvador, or one of his men, assuming he had servants. Even then it did not necessarily follow that he knew the identity of the man who had been coshed. He may have supposed him to be some casual Peeping Tom. He didn't want anyone near the place or he wouldn't have put up the notice 'No admittance'. It was dark at the time. If Maria had reported an intruder she may not have recognised Bertie. That went for Salvador himself, had he gone out.

The whole business was disturbing because it suggested that they themselves were being watched. Why? Did someone know what they were really doing there? Be that as it may, decided Biggles, the important thing was they now knew where Salvador lived. The next thing was to establish his identity. If it turned out that he was in fact Luis Salvador they could forget about him and continue the search for Neckel. That the *Intendente* knew no one of that name implied that the absconding scientist was living under an *alias*, anyhow. He was certainly in the district, or why should he have asked for letters to be addressed to him there? If it could be established that Salvador was Neckel then they could proceed with the task that had brought them to such an outlandish place.

Meanwhile, time was running out. A plan of some sort would have to be made without delay, and that meant chances would have to be taken. To wait for something to happen would lose more time. It would obviously be useless to approach Salvador direct. Nor did there seem any point in following him now they

knew where he lived. He would soon become suspicious
– if he wasn't already.

Boiled down it seemed that two lines of investigation
were open. Dolores and Maria. How much did they
know about Salvador? That could only be ascertained
by questioning them. Dolores could not be expected to
talk willingly; but money might buy her. With Maria it
was different. If, as there was reason to suppose, she was
a jealous woman, she might talk out of pique.

Bertie had dropped off to sleep, so Biggles got up and
quietly left the room. Downstairs he found the *patron* in
his untidy little sitting room and put the question to him:
had he a man who would take a message to Don Pedro?
He would go himself but he did not want to leave his
friend for any length of time.

The *patron* said he understood that. How was Señor
Lissie? Biggles said he was much better. All he needed
now was rest. The *patron* said he had a boy who would
take the message with pleasure. Whereupon Biggles
wrote a short note in which he said they were having a
little trouble. Could José run over and help them to get
it sorted out? Addressing the envelope to Don Pedro at
the Villa Vanda Biggles handed it to the *patron* saying
he was going out for a walk but would be back for
lunch.

The *patron*, with the letter in his hand, went out the
back way to the yard. Biggles went out of the front door
into the *plaza*, noticing on the way that Dolores was not
at her desk. But it was still only seven o'clock.

CHAPTER 7

JOSÉ COMES IN USEFUL

For a minute or two Biggles was tempted to wait for Dolores to come in and try his luck with her, for he was sure she could tell him quite a lot if she could be persuaded to talk; and he thought she would do that if it was made worth her while. Whether or not she would tell the truth was another matter. She had told José she didn't know where Salvador lived, but in view of her visit to the Casa Floresta that was obviously a lie – unless of course that was her first visit. Not that Biggles held that against her. Making allowances for her upbringing and where she lived, she could not be judged too strictly.

There was one thing he was sure she must know, and that was if Salvador was Neckel, or had any connection with him. He worked it out like this. She had told José she collected Salvador's letters at the post-office and took them to him. Why was that necessary? If the letters were addressed to Luis Salvador why didn't he collect them himself? Was the answer because the letters were addressed to someone else? Neckel, for instance. Air Commodore Raymond had said that a letter was being sent to Neckel to say his proposal was under consideration. That letter would certainly be addressed to

Mr Harald Neckel. Neckel would be expecting a letter
from London. How could he collect it without going to
the post-office? He would send someone else. Was this
what Dolores was doing?

Again, how much, if anything, did the girl know
about the assault on Bertie? She couldn't have been far
away at the time. She told the police she had found
Bertie lying in the street. Was this really the first she
knew about the affair, or did she know, from being at
the Casa Floresta, that the attack was intended? Was
her finding of Bertie part of a scheme arranged by Salvador?

Deciding that Dolores could be dealt with later, either
by himself or José, Biggles walked on down the now
almost deserted street. He passed the Bar Francisco,
now closed. It reminded him of the dancer, Maria, who
in some way appeared to be associated with Salvador. If
he had dropped her in favour of Dolores she might be in
a mood to talk if she thought it would embarrass him.
But that, too, could wait. The first thing was to have a
look at the place where Bertie had been attacked. It was
important to know who had been responsible for that,
for if it turned out to be Salvador it would imply he was
suspicious of them.

He had no difficulty whatever in finding the junction
of the two tracks as it had been described by Bertie. But
even before that he perceived that footprints were not
likely to tell him much, if anything, for the mud was
trampled by such marks, both male and female, going in
both directions.

A small area of disturbed ground on the nearside of

the fork he took to be the actual spot where Bertie had fallen. It was surrounded by footmarks. One set, deeply imprinted, were conspicuous. They showed a lattice-work sole of cane or straw, or some such material. He thought these might have been made by the person who had lifted Bertie's body, presumably the assailant, and carried it to the town, or at least to the near end of the main street. But this he knew was the type of footwear, a sort of home-made moccasin, commonly worn by the poorer sorts of people in the district; so apart from the fact that they came up the narrow track, evidently from the house, they told him nothing.

All was quiet. Under the forest trees it was still dim twilight. There was not a soul about, so he made a close examination of the place, thinking he might perhaps came across some object that had been dropped by the attacker; but he found nothing. He considered recon-noitring the house, the Casa Floresta, while he was there; but he did not proceed with it, fearing that if he was seen he was likely to do more harm than good. So, abandon-ing the search, he made his way back to the town, de-ciding on the way to try his luck with Maria, if she was available for an interview. She, he was sure, would be as interested in money as Dolores. He would at least test her reactions to a few questions. He realised that the dancing girl did not necessarily live at the Bar Fran-cisco, in which case there should be no difficulty in learn-ing where she was to be found. If she refused to talk – well, that would be that. If she was on visiting terms with Salvador she would know something about his private life. There was an obvious danger that she would tell Salvador that questions were being asked about him, but that was a risk he was now prepared to take. He had his excuse for the interview ready.

He found the establishment open, and as it turned out Maria was there.

A man, the sinister-looking individual who had been serving behind the bar the previous night, was mopping the floor in a desultory manner. In a dirty singlet, pants, and a pair of sloppy slippers, unshaven and unwashed, he presented an even less attractive picture. However, he was polite enough when Biggles, after wishing him a cheerful *buenos dias*, said he had called to see Maria, if that were possible. Leaning on his mop the man looked curious but refrained from asking why. He said Maria was his daughter. She was upstairs. He would ask her to come down.

In due course Maria appeared. In the cold light of day she looked very different from what she had in the soft lamplight. In fact, she looked such a drab, heavy-eyed creature that Biggles felt sorry for her in the life she had to lead, dancing every night before a crowd of drunken *llaneros*. He asked her to sit down and invited her to have a drink. She said she would have a beer. Her father brought it.

'I have come because I think you may be able to help me, *señorita*,' began Biggles, frankly. 'Last night I was here in the bar —'

'Yes. I saw you.'

'Sitting near me was a friend.' Biggles smiled. 'You sat on his lap – remember?'

Maria scowled. 'He threw me away.'

'He meant no offence. He is afraid of women.'

'Why?'

'I don't know. Some men are like that. But the point is this. After leaving here he decided to take a walk for some fresh air. Someone hit him on the head and he was injured. I am trying to find out who struck him, and more particularly, for what reason. He had no quarrel with anyone.'

Maria raised her hands, palms upwards. 'What is remarkable about this? It happens all the time. Was he robbed?'

'Yes.'

'Why should you think I know anything about this?'

'I thought you may have heard something about it. He was left lying in the street.'

'This is the first I have heard of it.'

'You didn't see anyone about last night who might have done it?'

'I didn't go out last night, so how could I have seen anyone?' lied the girl, brazenly.

'I thought I saw you go out with Señor Salvador,' suggested Biggles.

'I don't know this man,' declared Maria.

'He was in here last night.'

'So were many people. I don't know everyone.'

'I thought if Señor Salvador was a regular customer he might —'

'I have never heard of this Salvador,' insisted Maria, rudely, and getting up strode away into the back regions.

Biggles realised he had wasted his time, and may have done more harm than good. It was obvious he would learn nothing from Maria, who to his certain knowledge had lied from start to finish of the conversation. Why? Why had she denied all knowledge of Salvador? Was she trying to protect him? He came to the conclusion that however jealous she might be of Dolores, and in spite of the row which Bertie had witnessed, she was in love with the man. The alternative was he was paying her well to keep her mouth shut about anything she might know.

Biggles got up, paid for the drink and returned to the hotel. Dolores was in her usual place. She gave him a smile, which he returned, and went on upstairs to find Bertie out of bed taking some soup which the *patron* had brought him. He was obviously much better, and his question 'Any luck?' was in his normal voice.

'Nothing doing,' answered Biggles. 'I found nothing of interest at the place where you were coshed. On the way back I saw Maria, but all I got out of her was a string of lies. Either she's in love with Salvador or she's too scared to talk.' Biggles grinned. 'Or maybe she just didn't like the look of me. I sent a message to Don Pedro before I went out, asking if he could send José along. If he's coming he should soon be here. As you seem to be all right I'll go down and wait for him.'

'Okay, old boy. I shall probably come down myself presently.'

Biggles went down, and taking one of the chairs beside a row of small tables under an awning, settled down to wait.

About half an hour later, to his relief, José appeared on his pony. He rode into the yard. Biggles followed him, and having seen the pony tethered took the Negro to a shady corner.

'I need your help again, *compadre*,' he said seriously, and went on to tell of Bertie's misadventure. 'I want to know who did it, and for what reason,' he continued. 'I have a suspicion that this man Salvador knows something about it. I don't think Salvador is his real name. He reminds me of a crook known to the police in England. Dolores seems to know him well so I want you to speak to her again. It was she who found Señor Lissie lying unconscious on the path last night. Find out if she knows anything about it. Try to find out the name on the letters she collects at the post-office for Salvador. It may not be Salvador. Be careful how you ask the questions. Pretend it isn't important. Find out anything she knows about Salvador. You understand?'

'*Si, señor.* But dis man Salvador does everything like a man of this country.'

'So he may, but if he's the man I think he is his parents came from Europe. Do you think Dolores will talk to you?'

'Sure. We bin good friends long time.'

Biggles took out his wad of notes and handed some to José. 'Take these. Some money may help. I'll wait here. There's no hurry.'

'I find out everything,' promised José, optimistically, and walked off.

Biggles lit a cigarette and prepared to wait.

It was some time before José came back, but when he

did a broad smile suggested success. And so it transpired.

'Dolores tell me everything,' he said proudly, as he
walked up. 'She collects letters for a man name of
Neckel. Salvador tells Dolores dis man Neckel friend of
his.'

Biggles could hardly repress a smile of satisfaction.
So he had been right. Not for an instant did he believe
this tale about a friend. Salvador was Neckel. But it
would have to be confirmed. There was just a chance
that Neckel was hiding in the Casa Floresta as a guest of
Salvador.

'Letter comes for Neckel today,' went on José. 'Come
from England.'

'How do you know it came from England?'

'I see English stamp.'

'Did Dolores show you the letter?'

'Sure. She takes it Casa Floresta tonight.'

'Why isn't she meeting Salvador at the Bar Francisco
as usual?'

'Because trouble with Maria. Two women always
make trouble. Dolores she don' want to see Maria no
more.'

Biggles nodded. 'I can understand that. Maria thinks
Dolores has taken Salvador away from her.'

'Das right.'

'What else does Dolores know?'

'She swear to me de first thing she knows about
Señor Lissie is when she finds him lying beside road at
top end of street. She nearly falls over him.'

'What was she doing there?'

'She says she's bin to house with Salvador. Calls it Casa Floresta.'

I happen to know that's true, anyway. Then she doesn't know who hit Señor Lissie?'

'No, sah.'

'She didn't see anyone about?'

'She say the only man she sees near house was Carlo, a coloured man Salvador has there to keep people away. He don' like people near house.'

'Anything else?'

'No, *señor*. Das de lot.'

'Thank you, José. You've done splendidly. Dolores must like you.'

José grinned. 'She like me plenty. We old friends.'

'Why don't you marry her?'

José sighed. 'Don Pedro won't have no women about de place.'

'Did you give Dolores the money?'

'Sure. She mighty happy. Buy new dress, better than Maria.'

'Good. And what are you going to do now?'

'Don Pedro no want me back straight away. If you want me I stay. Mebbe go back tomorrow.'

Biggles smiled. 'You mean you're staying in town for a little while so that you can see Dolores again.'

José showed his white teeth in another grin. 'Das right, *señor*.'

'In that case you may learn something more about Salvador. I'll see you again before you go.'

'*Si, señor*.' José strolled away.

Deep in thought Biggles watched him walk out into

the *plaza*. So that was it, he mused. It now seemed almost certain that Salvador was Neckel. If that was correct it seemed equally certain that the missing documents were somewhere in the Casa Floresta. The next problem was how to get them, for no doubt they would be carefully hidden.

He made his way to the bar where he found Bertie, his head still bandaged of course, sitting at one of the small tables with a long drink at his elbow. Joining him he related the information he had just received from José.

'Jolly good.' said Bertie. 'What's the next move?'

'I don't think we can do anything more for the moment. I'd like to have a look at this Casa Floresta, but apparently Salvador keeps a guard on duty and if he spotted me prowling about it might start something, in which case I'd have done more harm than good. A better plan, I think, would be for me to follow Dolores when she goes there tonight with that letter, to watch what happens.'

'Don't forget what happened to me.'

'I shall keep that in mind, you may be sure. I should be able to see where Dolores goes when she gets there. With luck I might even be able to overhear a conversation. That letter from England, by the way, must be the one the Air Commodore told me was being sent. It would be interesting to see how Salvador reacts when he reads it. He won't waste any time doing that, because if I know the type he must be pretty sick of hanging around in this dead-and-alive hole. I admit this all sounds a bit vague, but I can't think of anything else we can do for the moment. If I learn nothing tonight I shall have to risk exploring in daylight. I shall have to get the layout of the place in my mind before there can be any question of breaking in.'

'You think it'll come to that?'

'We've got to get those papers, and they won't come to us. I can't imagine Salvador walking about with them in his pocket. If I thought that I'd have no compunction in going to any length to take them off him. They're British Government property, and he stole them.'

'True enough, old boy. I'm with you there.'

'How are you feeling now?'

'Not too bad. By tonight I should be fit enough to come with you, if you think I might help.'

'No thanks.' Biggles was emphatic. 'You're staying at home until you're absolutely fit; and you may have to be before this job is finished. Anything can happen.' Biggles got up. 'Let's go through and have some lunch.'

DEATH INTERVENES

THE rest of the day passed quietly. The only thing that happened was a visit from the *Intendente* to see how Bertie was getting on and to say he had been unable to find the man who had knocked him down. In the circumstances this came as no surprise to Biggles, but he did not say so. The great thing was they were still on good terms with the official, whose help they might need before the end of their assignment. They drank some wine together.

After that there was nothing to do until nightfall, when Dolores might be expected to take the letter to the Casa Floresta.

When that time came Biggles did not go to the Bar Francisco, this being unnecessary. Knowing which way the girl must go to get to the house he walked along the track until he was just short of the fork and then settled down to wait, knowing she would have to pass him. He found a comfortable spot in some ferns close to the track, which was all he could do. It proved to be a long and tiresome business, with the mosquitoes a nuisance, although this was to be expected.

The night was hot and dark, and starlight hardly penetrating the canopy of leaves overhead. The air was heavy with humidity, and apart from the hum of the mosquitoes and an occasional stealthy rustling in the forest, silence reigned, a profound hush as if everything was waiting for something to happen. Time dragged along on leaden feet as it usually does when one is keyed up yet forced to keep still.

It must have been nearly eleven when Biggles heard the sound for which he had waited for so long: the quick pad of footsteps on soft earth. A shadowy figure loomed, walking so quickly that it passed on in a moment, before there could be any question of recognition. In the gloom this would have been difficult, anyway. All Biggles could be sure of was that it was a woman, so he could only assume, with a fair amount of confidence, that it was Dolores, on her way to the Casa Floresta with the letter. It was disconcerting not to know definitely that it was her, but for that, in such conditions, he was prepared. There was no way of overcoming that difficulty. Anyhow, he was sure few women used the track at that hour of night.

In a moment he was out of his hiding place, listening intently, hoping that by the soft patter of footsteps he would be able to confirm that the nocturnal traveller had taken the left fork to the house. He could see nothing.

Then, as he stood there, from a little way ahead there came sounds that stiffened his muscles and set his nerves quivering. There was a gasp, a scream that ended in a moan, and a thud as if someone had fallen. An instant later he could hear swift footsteps approaching.

He flung himself back into the ferns just in time. He caught a fleeting glimpse of a black-draped figure running towards the town, but could not tell who it was. It had gone in a flash.

For some seconds he lay still. Not until the footsteps had faded away did he move. Then, rising to his feet, he stared, eyes trying to probe the darkness, up and down the track, braced for a quick move should the necessity arise. He could hear no sound. Nothing stirred. The forest had resumed its sinister silence. What had happened? Such a scream could only mean tragedy. The very atmosphere seemed suddenly brittle with foreboding. Who had done what, to whom? Wiping sweat and mosquitoes from his forehead with his sleeve, with his heart thumping uncomfortably, he advanced slowly, a step at a time, towards the fork, a mere yard or two farther on. It was from there, he judged, that the scream had come.

A few paces and his questing eyes made out a long dark object lying across the track. Another step and doubt departed. It was a body. A skirt told him it was a woman. Again for a moment he stood tense, looking up and down and trying to peer into the dark jungle on either side; then, kneeling beside the body he felt it with his hands, hoping to learn something. He did. She was lying face down, and he caught his breath sharply as they came into contact with an object protruding from her back. It was a handle; the handle of a knife, or a blade of some sort.

Still he could not see who she was. Taking out his petrol lighter he flicked it on. The feeble flame told him what he wanted to know. It was Dolores. That she was dead he did not doubt, for a stiletto had been driven in to the hilt and must have pierced her heart. Her dress, bright blue, looked new. The thought struck Biggles that this must be the one she had bought with the money José had given her. She had bought it to compete with Maria for Salvador's affection. Poor kid, he thought. He had no great regard for the girl, but he was conscious of a sudden flood of pity. Whatever her character might be she did not deserve this.

He turned the body over. In doing this he exposed a small, white square object. He picked it up. It was a letter, the one, presumably, she had collected at the post-office, and was on her way to deliver to Salvador. Apparently she had been carrying it in her hand, and had dropped it when she had been struck. He looked at the address. The envelope was smeared with blood, but he could make out the name; Mr H. Neckel, and a post-office number at Cruzuado. The stamp was British. He put the letter in his pocket. The contents at that moment did not interest him. He could guess what they were. Without touching the fatal blade he lifted the body to the side of the track, and replacing the lighter in his pocket stood motionless, wondering what he should do in a situation far removed from anything he could have imagined. Now that the first shock had passed he was able to think; and he saw he had plenty to think about. His own position was a dangerous one, or it would be if someone came along and saw him standing by the body, still limp and not yet cold in death.

He thought fast. Who had killed the girl? He was

almost sure it was a woman, for he fancied he had caught the swish of skirts as the figure had rushed past him on the way to the town. Maria, of course, was the first person to come to his mind. She had a motive. Jealousy. They had quarrelled, and the stiletto had been used with hatred behind the blow. The awful thought struck him that he might unwittingly have been re- sponsible for the girl's death. She had talked. Perhaps said too much to José. If that had become known she might have been murdered for that reason. But some- how he did not think that was the answer. It seemed far more likely that if Maria had known, or guessed, that Dolores was going to the Casa Floresta, she might well have decided to dispose of her rival once and for all. It would have been a simple matter to lie in wait for her, and coming up behind her stab her as she went past. Biggles did not overlook that he was in a country where blood ran hot, and murder was a common event. Or so he had been told.

With his brain racing it was clear he would have to make up his mind what he was going to do. And quickly. Three courses he could see were open to him. The first was to put himself in the clear by going away and saying nothing to anybody about what he had seen and heard. That would be the easy way out. But he did not entertain the idea for long. It was too utterly callous. He could not bring himself to leave the girl lying there, probably until daylight the next day, a prey to any ver- min that might come along. After all, she had helped him. Moreover she was a close friend of José.

The second course open was to go on to the Casa

Floresta and report what had happened to Salvador – to give the man his assumed name – leaving him to do anything he might consider advisable. But Biggles didn't care much for that plan, either. The third and last course was to go at once to the *Intendente* and tell him about the tragedy, saying he was out for a walk and had come across the body by accident, which in a way was not far from the truth. This, he felt, as a police officer himself, was the right thing to do. Indeed, if only out of respect for the dead girl he couldn't see how he could do anything else.

But how much should he tell the *Intendente*? That was the question. To tell him all he knew, or suspected, could hardly fail to complicate his own affairs. That would certainly happen if he handed over the letter Dolores had been carrying when she met her death. It was addressed to Neckel. The *Intendente* would read it, and putting two and two together, associate with Neckel his own purpose in being in the town. He recalled he had already mentioned Neckel's name to him. No, decided Biggles. That wouldn't do. It would be better to say nothing about the letter, which had no bearing on the case beyond the fact that it would account for Dolores being on her way to the Casa Floresta.

There was another angle. If he reported his suspicion to the *Intendente*, that Dolores had been murdered by Maria, word would get around, and her relations, holding him responsible for her arrest, would make his position in Cruzuado untenable. As likely as not he would be the next one to get a knife in his back some dark night.

Having made up his mind, he set off at a fast pace for the office of the Chief of Police. To his relief he met no one until he was in the main street. Passing the Bar Francisco, from which regardless of the hour there still came the customary noise of revelry, he put his head in the door and saw Maria doing her usual dance act. That, he realised, didn't mean she had not been out.

Continuing on his way he was soon at the police head-quarters, to be informed by the *agente* on duty that the *Intendente* had just gone to bed.

'Then I must ask you to fetch him, for a matter I have to report is both urgent and important,' requested Biggles.

After a short delay the *Intendente* appeared.

'I'm sorry to disturb you at this hour, but there is something you should know, *señor*,' began Biggles.

'I am at your service,' stated the officer courteously, but looking puzzled.

'A short while ago I went for a walk before going to bed. It took me a little way beyond the top end of the street, almost to the place where the road goes in two directions.'

'I know it. You mean where your friend was attacked and robbed?'

'Exactly, *señor*. There, lying across the road, I found the body of a girl. She had been stabbed to death.'

The police officer grimaced. 'Did you recognise her?'

'Yes. With my cigarette lighter I saw it was the girl from my hotel, the one they call Dolores.'

The *Intendente* clicked his tongue.

'The knife was in her back. I didn't touch it, but I moved the body to the side of the road; then I came straight back to tell you.'

'Now what *demonio* has done this?' muttered the *Intendente*. 'Did you see the person?'

'No, *señor*. It is true I saw someone running down the road, but it was dark so I couldn't say who it was.'

The policeman sighed. 'I get no peace. Very well, *señor*. I will attend to it.'

'In that case I shall go to bed. Should you want me I shall be in the hotel.'

'Gracias. Buenas noches, señor.'

'Adios.'

Biggles retired to the hotel, and to his room, where he found Bertie waiting for him.

Bertie took one look at his face and asked: 'What's happened?'

'Dolores has been murdered.'

'Oh no!'

'It's true. I went along to the fork in the road to wait for her to pass, as I told you I would. She came along, and within a minute went down with a knife in her back.' Biggles went on to narrate in detail exactly what had happened.

'What a shocker! What did you do about it?'

'I came back and told the *Intendente*. What else could I do?'

'Nothing, old boy. I can see that. How much did you tell the police?'

'Not more than I had to, you may be sure of that. The last thing we want is to be mixed up in a murder case.'

'Who did it, do you think? Maria?'

'It looks that way to me; but I've no proof.'

'Did you give the letter to the police?'

'No. I said nothing about it. I have an idea for putting it to better use.'

'Have you opened it?'

'No. It's addressed to Neckel, not to Salvador, and that's all I need to know. If, as I suppose, it's the letter the Air Commodore said was being sent from London there's no point in opening it. We know what it's about.'

'What are you going to do with it?'

'I'm thinking of taking it along to Neckel, first thing in the morning.'

'That's taking a chance.'

'The time has come when we shall have to take chances. Delivering the letter will enable me to have a close look at Salvador in daylight, and perhaps provide an opportunity to see inside the house.'

Bertie thought for a moment. 'Has it occurred to you to wonder what José is going to say about this?'

'It has.'

'You haven't told him?'

'I don't know where to look for him. He's sleeping somewhere in the town and no doubt he'll be along in the morning. I shall probably have gone by then so it will be up to you to tell him, if he hasn't already heard the news.'

'He may cut up rough. He was fond of that girl.'

'I know, but there's nothing I can do about it. It's happened. And there it is.'

'He'll guess it was Maria. He knew Dolores was on bad terms with her.'

'What if he does? He can do what he likes as far as I'm concerned as long as he doesn't drag us into it.'

'It's a bad show.'

'Are you telling me! But let's sleep on it. We may feel better about it in the morning.'

CHAPTER 9

BOGOSOFF SHOWS
HIS HAND

THE morning broke fine, the sky pale blue beyond patches of thin mist, already lifting, promising another hot day.

It found Biggles on the move early, which awakened Bertie, who declared he was back to normal and suggested he accompanied Biggles to the Casa Floresta. Biggles had confirmed his intention of paying a visit to Salvador, the letter in his pocket providing an excuse not to be wasted.

But Biggles would not have it. He said he could manage the affair alone, so it would be better for Bertie to concentrate on getting absolutely fit before trying to do too much too soon, and so possibly bring on a relapse at a time when all his stamina would really be needed.

'You stick around the hotel to deal with anything that might arise while I'm away,' he ordered. 'If you see José you can tell him what has happened to Dolores, but don't say more than is necessary. See how he takes it. He's bound to be upset. If I see him downstairs or in the yard I'll tell him myself.'

'What if the *Intendente* comes round asking for you?'

'Tell him I've gone out but you expect me back for

lunch. Better not tell him where I've gone or he may wonder what business I have with Salvador. In fact, to prevent him from getting suspicious as to why we're hanging about here for so long, you might drop the word that we're thinking of joining Don Pedro at the Villa Vanda very soon now. Incidentally, that's true, because it's time we had a look at the machine to make sure she's all right. At any time now we might need her in a hurry.'

'Okay, old boy. But if the police are going to get suspicious of anyone, what about Bogosoff? Have you seen him lately?'

'No.'

'What do you suppose has happened to him?'

'I haven't a clue. I imagine he's still around, and I have a feeling he's not here for his health; but I shan't waste time looking for him while he keeps out of our way. See you later.' Biggles left the room.

It so happened that the first person he saw when he went out to the *plaza* was José, leaning against a hitching rail. 'Hello, what are you doing here?' he asked, after the usual *'Buenos dias.'*

José, always cheerful, grinned as he admitted he was waiting for Dolores to arrive. He had a little present for her.

'Then I shall have to give you some bad news,' returned Biggles, sadly. 'Dolores won't be coming here any more.'

'Not come back?' José looked astonished.

'You'll have to know the truth, *amigo*. Prepare for a shock. Dolores is dead.'

'*Dead?*'

'Last night she was murdered.'

Biggles never forgot the expression on José's face. The smile seemed to freeze into a mask. His lips became thin lines drawn hard against white teeth. His hands opened and closed, slowly. For an uncomfortable moment Biggles thought the Negro was going to spring at him. But the fear passed when José said, softly but with a dangerous edge on his voice: 'Who kill my gal?'

Biggles shook his head. 'I don't know.'

'Maria.' José breathed the word.

'I said I didn't know.'

'Salvador. He's de man don' dis. De gals was frens till he come.'

'I'd rather not express an opinion on that.'

'Who tell you dis?'

'Unfortunately I found Dolores' body myself. Late last night I walked up the street to watch if she went to the Casa Floresta. She went past me. She didn't see me. Presently I heard a scream and hurried along to see what had happened. She was lying on the ground with a knife in her back.'

'You see who don' it?'

'No. Some person ran past me, but it was very dark so I couldn't make out who it was.'

'What you do?'

'The only thing I could do. When I realised she was dead I hurried back to tell the *Intendente*. I haven't seen him since, but I imagine he sent men to bring in the body.'

'Where dey take her?'

'I don't know. You'll have to ask the police. I went to bed when I left the office of the *Intendente*.'

There was a short but uncomfortable silence.

'I kill someone for dis,' said José thickly, his hand to his machete. Then to Biggles' embarrassment tears began rolling down the black face so often wreathed in a smile.

Biggles pushed some money in his hand. 'Go inside and have a drink,' he advised. 'At a time like this a man needs one. It'll pull you together. Do nothing in a hurry. Señor Lissie will be down presently. He'll talk to you. The *Intendente* may come along, and no doubt he'll tell you what he's been able to find out.'

With his head bowed the Negro walked away and into the hotel.

Biggles sighed as he continued on his way, relieved that the man had taken the grim news as well as he had.

There were now a few people in the street, but no one he knew, and when he reached the track he found it deserted. He walked with eyes and ears alert, for in view of all that had happened on it the place had acquired an ugly character. When he came to the fork he paused to look around. The body of the dead girl was of course no longer there. Seeing nothing of interest he walked on, quite openly, towards the house, the Casa Floresta, his eyes taking in the details.

He stopped at the gate. Or rather, he was stopped by a

big, ugly half-breed, who was evidently there for that purpose.

'What you want, man?' he was asked, curtly.

'I've come to see Señor Salvador.'

'He don't see no one.'

'I think he'll see me if you'll tell him I have news for him, and a letter,' returned Biggles, evenly.

'Wait.' Scowling, the man walked to the house, which stood a little way back.

Biggles took the opportunity to have a good look at it.

Presently the man reappeared. Without a word he opened the gate. Biggles followed him to the door, where he was met by the man he had come to see. Even before he spoke Salvador had to take a cigarette from his lips to cough.

'You wanted to see me?' he inquired, politely, in a voice in which there was just a trace of transatlantic accent.

'I have a letter which may have been intended for you, or for a friend of yours.'

'Indeed. How did you get it?'

'It came into my possession in unusual, not to say tragic, circumstances. I thought you might like to hear about it.'

'Come in.'

Biggles followed Salvador into a simply furnished but pleasant sitting room.

'Please be seated,' requested Salvador. 'Can I get you some refreshment?'

'No thanks. I've only just had my breakfast. As you

are probably aware, I'm staying with a friend of mine at the Hotel Comisaria. We're here to arrange new contracts with an Englishman who lives a little way down the river. He's known locally as Don Pedro. He's an orchid collector.'

'As a matter of fact I did hear something of the sort,' answered Salvador carelessly. 'I once saw you in a bar in the town.'

'The Bar Francisco.'

'That's right.'

'I saw you there, too. You were with the reception clerk at our hotel, a girl named Dolores.'

'Possibly.'

'That's one of the reasons why I've come to see you. As apparently you were friendly with her I thought you'd be interested to know she was murdered last night not far from this house. Did you know that?'

Salvador's expression had changed. 'No.'

'Late last night I went for a stroll before turning in. On the track that comes this way after leaving the town I came across a body lying on the ground. I hadn't a torch, but using my petrol lighter I saw it was Dolores. There was a knife in her back. In moving her to the side of the track I found a letter lying on the ground. It struck me that if she was a friend of yours she might have been on her way here. My first thought was to go to the nearest house, presumably yours, for help, but I decided that as the girl was dead nothing could be done for her and it would be better to inform the police.'

'Did you do that?'

'Yes. I told the *Intendente*, and was able to tell him the identity of the victim.'

'Did you give him the letter?' asked Salvador, sharply.

'No. I had put it in my pocket and had forgotten about it by the time I got to him. Anyway, obviously it was not the motive for the murder or the murderer would have taken it. I remembered it when I got up this morning, so thinking it might be a purely personal matter I've brought it along to see if it was intended for you. It may not be. I understand your name is Salvador, and the letter is addressed to someone named Neckel.'

'Neckel is a friend of mine. He sometimes stays here with me,' was the quick explanation.

'In that case you'd better have it.'

Biggles handed over the bloodstained envelope. After a glance at it Salvador put it in his pocket. 'Thank you,' he said. 'I'm most grateful to you. It couldn't in any way be connected with the murder. The simple fact is this. Rather than make unnecessary journeys into the town I asked this poor girl to inquire every day at the post-office, and if there was any mail for either Salvador or Neckel to bring it along here when she had finished her work at the hotel. As a matter of detail I gave her a little money for her trouble. That explains why she was on her way here, with this particular letter, when she was murdered.'

'So that was it,' murmured Biggles. 'I thought it might be something of the sort.'

Salvador, coughing periodically, was rolling another

cigarette. He wore no signet ring, but seeing the man in broad daylight, visualising him without the beard, Biggles was no longer in any doubt about his real identity. He was satisfied that this was Neckel, the absconding scientist.

'Did you by any chance see the man who murdered this unfortunate girl?' inquired Neckel.

'I did see someone, in a hurry, but it was too dark for me to recognise the person. I don't think it was a man. It seemed to me to be a woman. Anyhow, that's the impression I got.'

'Ah,' breathed Neckel, with a curious significance that was not lost on Biggles. 'You have absolutely no idea as to who she was?'

'It wouldn't be true to say that.'

'Then who do you *think* it might have been?'

'I couldn't swear to it, but from her figure, or something about her, as she ran past me in the dark I thought it might be the girl I'd seen dancing in the Bar Francisco.'

'Did she see you?'

'I don't think so. If she did she could hardly have recognised me.'

'Did you tell the *Intendente* about this?'

'No.'

'Why not?'

'Frankly, because I'd rather not be involved. I've lived long enough to learn to mind my own business. I'm only a visitor, and the affair has nothing to do with me.'

'How wise of you. When you see him again may I ask

you to say nothing about the letter, my reason for that being the same as yours. The letter can have no possible connection with the reason for the murder, I do assure you of that. Taking it all in all, the less said the better.'

'As you wish. I did of course tell the *Intendente* where I'd seen the body, so although he did not say so there is a chance that his inquiries may bring him here. That's why I came along early, so that the news, when it reached you through the police, should not come as a shock.'

'Thank you. That was very considerate of you.' Neckel got up, a plain hint that the interview was at an end.

Biggles, too, had got to his feet, satisfied with the successful outcome of a visit that had told him what he wanted to know, when from outside, close at hand, came the sound of voices raised high; one it seemed, in protest. This was cut short by the report of a firearm. There were quick footsteps in the hall, and into the room marched Bogosoff, an automatic held in front of him.

'Keep still, both of you,' he ordered harshly. Glancing at Biggles he went on: 'Keep out of this and you'll come to no harm.' Then, to Neckel, he snapped: 'Where are the papers? Hand them over. Don't argue or you'll get what your man outside has got.'

Neckel half turned towards the open window as if contemplating escape, whereupon Bogosoff continued: 'You can't get away. I've a man outside and he'd as soon shoot you as look at you.'

Biggles looked at Neckel. Feigning ignorance he asked, really to gain time, for he knew the answer perfectly well: 'What's all this about?'

To which Neckel replied: 'I don't know. The man must be mad.'

Biggles was watching his eyes, knowing, or hoping, they would turn subconsciously to the place where the papers were hidden, if they were in the room.

'Come on,' rapped out Bogosoff, with iron in his voice. 'I haven't got all day.'

Neckel's tongue flicked over his lips. All colour had fled from his face. He looked like a cornered rat. He glanced at Biggles appealingly as he sank, trembling, into a chair.

Biggles would have helped him had he been able to do so, for the last thing he wanted was to see the documents pass into the hands of Bogosoff, who now stood revealed as an enemy agent. But in such a situation, with the other man holding a gun which he was obviously prepared to use, there was nothing he could do.

'You've got five seconds,' said Bogosoff. 'I'm giving you a chance. If necessary I can find the papers myself, if I have to tear the house to pieces.'

'All right,' said Neckel in a hollow voice. 'I'll have to fetch them.'

This, Biggles observed, was a change of tune. Neckel no longer protested that he didn't know to what papers Bogosoff was referring. That implied they were somewhere in the house.

'Where are they?' asked Bogosoff.

'In my bedroom.'

'Lead the way. I'll come with you. Try no tricks or I'll shoot you as you deserve, you dirty traitor.'

This apparently was a reference to Neckel leaving his job behind the Iron Curtain for the West.

Sweat was running down Neckel's ashen face. From his expression he expected to be shot anyway, for daring to betray his previous employers. He would know as well as anyone that he could expect no mercy from them.

'I'll give you the papers if you'll promise not to kill me,' he faltered.

Biggles smiled faintly at the thought of what such a promise would be worth, even if it were given.

How the matter would have ended is a matter for conjecture, but at that moment there came an interruption which, as far as Biggles was concerned, came as a welcome respite. It must have been a great relief to Neckel, too. There was nothing really remarkable about it. In fact, it might have been expected.

From the garden came voices, then footsteps at the door. Into the room walked the *Intendente* with one of his policemen. 'Who shot that man outside?' he asked, crisply.

On seeing who the visitors were Bogosoff had lost no time in putting the pistol in his pocket. But he was not quite quick enough, and the *Intendente* must have seen it, for he said sharply: 'Was it you?'

'I know nothing about a dead man,' answered Bogosoff. 'Ask him.' He pointed at Neckel.

'He's lying,' shouted Neckel excitedly. 'He killed my

servant and was just going to shoot me when you came.'

Bogosoff waited for no more. Before anything could be done to prevent it he had jumped past the police officers and in a moment was out of the house. Through the window Biggles could see him racing down the slope towards the river. His companion, the man he had left outside, followed hard on his heels. They scrambled into the canoe, cast off and were away.

The police officers had not stood idle while this was going on. They, too, had run out, and standing on the grass fired several shots at the men in the canoe. Excusably they failed to hit their target, which was soon at extreme range for pistol shooting.

The *Intendente* came back into the house, where Biggles was standing watching Neckel pour himself a stiff drink with hands that so trembled that as much spirit missed the glass as went into it. Neither of them had spoken. Biggles could think of nothing to say, and Neckel was obviously suffering too much from shock for explanations.

'What has been going on here?' asked the *Intendente*, looking suspiciously at them in turn.

'I'll leave him to tell you,' answered Biggles, indicating Neckel. This, he decided quickly, was the easiest way out. Neckel could do the explaining. He wanted no part in what seemed likely to be a difficult situation.

'What brought you here?' the police officer asked Biggles.

'I merely walked along to tell Señor Salvador what

had happened near his house last night. I thought he would like to know. That's all. I found him engaged.'

'All right. You may go. I'll deal with this,' decided the *Intendente,* much to Biggles' relief.

Biggles went out and walked quickly towards the town.

CHAPTER 10

COMPLICATIONS

BIGGLES walked to the hotel somewhat worried by the
course events had taken but on the whole well satisfied
with the results of his visit to the Casa Floresta.

Much of the fog in which he had been groping had
been dispersed. As he had suspected, the man calling
himself Salvador was Neckel, and Bogosoff had proved
himself to be an enemy agent, in Cruzuado for the same
purpose as themselves. It seemed almost certain from
Neckel's behaviour that the stolen documents were in
the house. Bogosoff obviously thought so. Biggles had
the layout of the establishment in his mind's eye, and the
interior of at least one of the rooms. He had reason to
think the papers were in that room.

The big question was, in view of what had happened,
would the documents be allowed to remain there? For
that matter, would Neckel continue to live there? He
had had the fright of his life, and but for the opportune
arrival of the police would in all probability have lost
his life. Biggles would not have given much for his
chance had Bogosoff succeeded in getting his hands on
the papers. Another question was, what would Neckel
tell the *Intendente* to account for the situation in which
he had been found, with a dead man practically on the

doorstep? One thing that did seem clear was this; the business was fast coming to a head.

On walking into the hotel Biggles found Bertie the sole occupant of the bar, so taking a seat beside him he lost no time in telling him all that had transpired at the Casa Floresta.

When he had finished Bertie pursed his lips and whistled softly. 'Phew! I say! What a carry-on. This will certainly send the balloon up. What do we do next?'

'We shall have to do something, and quickly,' announced Biggles grimly. 'Things won't stay as they are for very long, you may be sure of that. Bogosoff got away, but he won't stay away. He was sent here to get those papers and he won't dare to go back to where he came from, wherever that may be, without them. Neckel, having lived behind the Iron Curtain for years, must know that as well as we do. From the way he looked and behaved when Bogosoff burst in, he thought he was going to be bumped off there and then – as no doubt he would have been had Bogosoff known where the papers were hidden. Neckel may have brains, but he has about as much guts as a rabbit. What I'm afraid of is, he'll bolt like one after what's happened. If he disappears we've had it. We could never hope to find him again; he'd take good care of that.'

'The *Intendente* must have supposed the man who was dead outside, apparently Neckel's bodyguard, had been shot by Bogosoff.'

'No doubt Neckel told him that I imagine it was true, anyway.'

'In that case Bogosoff won't dare to come back for fear of being arrested.'

'He might come back after dark, up the river. Incidentally, I believe the man who was shot was the fellow who clouted you. I had a look at him when I left the house and noticed he was wearing shoes that might have made certain footprints I saw at the spot where you were coshed.'

'If that's right I'm glad he got what was coming to him,' said Bertie.

'There's just one thing that might keep Neckel here.'

'What's that?'

'The letter I gave him. That is, if it says what the Air Commodore told me it would say. It was intended to gain time. It wouldn't flatly refuse Neckel's demand for a million dollars. It would say the matter was still under consideration. That would imply another letter, giving a definite decision, was to follow. Neckel would read it that way. All his plans must depend on whether or not the government is going to hand over the money; and the only way he can get to know that is by waiting for the next letter. If I'm right in this it means that Neckel, even if he leaves the Casa Floresta, will have to remain within easy reach of the post-office in Cruzuado.'

'He could send someone in for his letters.'

'Who? Dolores is dead. True, he might get someone else to go, but in order to arrange that he'd first have to go to the post-office himself. Methods here may be a bit slipshod, but I can't see the post-office handing over other people's letters to any Tom, Dick or Harry who walks in and asks for them.'

'I see what you mean. Queer how things work out. If Neckel hadn't asked Dolores to collect his letters she wouldn't have been murdered, and the whole story would have been different.'

'If it was Maria who stabbed Dolores it could have happened anyway. But never mind about the past. Let's stick to the present. I left the *Intendente* at the house talking to Neckel. What Neckel will tell him I can't imagine, but you can bet your boots he won't mention the papers that are at the bottom of it all. One thing that is certain is this: as soon as the *Intendente* leaves he'll get cracking.'

'Doing what?'

'That's what I'd like to know.'

'Moving the papers, perhaps.'

'Possibly, although they must be as safe where they are as anywhere.'

'While you were in the house did you get any indication of where they might be?'

'A very vague one. When Bogosoff barged in I watched Neckel's eyes, thinking they might for an instant switch involuntarily to the place where he kept them. That can happen, you know. He appeared to glance towards a picture on the wall. Quite a small one, but large enough to hide a wall safe. If I can get into the house that's the first thing I shall make for. There's a chance the papers may be there, or somewhere in that direction.'

'So the next step is to get into the house.'

'No. The first thing is to watch the house to see if Neckel leaves.'

'He might slip across the river to Brazil.'

'He can't do that without getting another water craft from somewhere. Bogosoff pinched his canoe, which I imagine was there for that purpose. If he decides to bolt he'll have to come here, into the town, for transport. He's not likely to get it anywhere else. Unless he's out of his mind he won't try going out through the jungle. By the way, how are you feeling?'

'Fine.'

'Good; because I shall have to ask you to keep an eye on the Casa Floresta to see if Neckel leaves. I can't do that myself because it's more than likely the *Intendente* will want to talk to me, either about the murder of Dolores or to check up on Neckel's story as to what was happening in the Casa Floresta this morning. He must be wondering what I was doing there. Tell me, did you see José?'

'Yes, he came in here. He said you'd told him about Dolores.'

'How did he shape?'

'Not too well. He kept saying he'd kill someone for this. He seemed to hold Salvador, as he calls him, responsible for throwing over Maria. He went across to the bar and settled down as if he was determined to drink himself to death. He was necking that local poison, *aguardiente*. He was here until about half an hour ago.'

'Bad show. Well, we had nothing to do with what went on between Maria and Dolores. He must realise that. I wonder where he went. He said he'd be going back to the Villa Vanda this morning. If he was in the state you say he was he'd do better to wait until tomorrow. I'll go and find out if he's gone. If his pony is still here he must still be in the town. I don't want him to run into the *Intendente*. He may talk too much. He knows about Dolores collecting Neckel's letters. He might say I'd bribed him to get information from Dolores about Neckel.'

'Hm. That's a point I hadn't thought of.'

'It's a point that could well start the *Intendente* thinking, and so make things difficult for us.'

'It might.'

'Stand fast while I have a look round.'

Biggles went out into the yard. There he found the stable-boy and from him learned that José's pony was still there. He didn't know where José had gone. He hadn't seen him for some time, when he had noticed him walking across the *plaza*.

Returning to Bertie Biggles said: 'I can't see him about, but his pony is still here, so it doesn't look as if he's gone back to the Villa Vanda.'

'He'll turn up,' replied Bertie. 'Probably gone to sleep off the effects of the *aguardiente*.'

'I hope you're right,' returned Biggles dubiously.

Further conjecture on the subject was cut short by the arrival of the *Intendente*, with the Comisario.

'We meet again, *señor*,' said the *Intendente*, cheerfully.

'What news this time?' inquired Biggles casually, but a little worried for fear the police officer was going to question him about what happened at the Casa Floresta.

The officer said he had only looked in to tell the *patron* that he had arrested the woman who had murdered his receptionist, Dolores.

Biggles frowned. 'Did you say a *woman*?'

'*Sir, señor.*'

'Who do you mean?'

'The one they call Maria. The girl who dances at the Bar Francisco. She's the daughter of the man who keeps the place.'

'What makes you think she did it?'

'I know.'

'How?'

'Señor Salvador told me so.'

'How does he know? Was he there?'

'No, but he knew all about it. He told me in his house this morning after you had gone.'

'He told you?' Biggles could hardly say the words without showing his disgust and contempt for the man.

'He admitted he hadn't actually seen the murder done,' went on the *Intendente*, as if the matter was of no great consequence. 'But Maria had told him she would do it one day. She has often been heard to say that. It was her stiletto that did the killing. There were still bloodstains on the sleeve of her dress when I arrested her. Presently she will confess. Ah! Here is the *patron*.' The three of them went through to the proprietor's private sitting room.

Biggles had no doubt that the police officer had

arrested the right person, but he was appalled by her betrayer's perfidy. He looked at Bertie white with anger. 'Did you hear that?'

'Of course.'

'What a complete swine Neckel must be. I'm pretty sure Maria did kill Dolores, but that's beside the point. What turns my stomach is that Neckel, who'd been carrying on with Maria, should go out of his way to rat on her. He must have volunteered the information that Maria had said she'd kill Dolores, which may or may not be true. He, of all people.'

'Why should he do it?'

'Not because he's concerned with justice, the yellow crook; you can bet your sweet life on that. It may have been to put himself on the right side of the *Intendente*, or more likely his way of getting rid of Maria for good now he's had enough of her. Great grief! What curs there are in the world.'

'Too true,' agreed Bertie, moodily. 'What effect is all this going to have on us?'

'I don't know. It's too soon to say. Maybe none. But it might upset our apple cart if Neckel told the *Intendente* that I'd seen a woman near the body of Dolores. Like a fool I admitted that to Neckel. The *Intendente* may wonder why I didn't tell him that. Again, if Maria or her relatives ever got to hear that I'd told Neckel I'd seen her near the spot they'd be after me with knives and guns. She was popular with the *llaneros*. The trouble is, I don't know how much Neckel told the police. It's pretty clear Maria didn't know much about Neckel's business here or he wouldn't have given her away for fear she spilt the beans. When I spoke to Maria she wouldn't say a word against Salvador, as she supposes his name to be.'

Bertie shook his head. 'It all strikes me as being a dirty business. This feller Neckel must be an absolute stinker, and the sooner someone bumps him off the better for everyone.'

'I couldn't agree more, but it isn't for us to do that. To get down to brass tacks, we now know as much as we're ever likely to know from the outside of the Casa Floresta. All that remains for us to do is get inside and find the papers. I'm not fooling myself that's likely to be easy. Apart from Neckel we still have Bogosoff to reckon with. We know why he's here, and he won't leave the district while he thinks there's the slightest chance of getting what he came for. Which reminds me. It's time you pressed on to the house to see what goes on. Don't go too close. All I want to know is if Neckel leaves the place, and if so which way he goes. I'll waffle along presently and join you, but for the moment I think I'd better stay here in case the *Intendente* wants to speak to me again. I'll try to find José. I'm a bit worried about him. I hope he doesn't do anything silly. It only needs him to kill somebody, or even start shouting about what he knows, to put sand in our gearbox.'

'If he got into trouble it'd be poor thanks to Don Pedro for lending him to us.'

'You're right. Whether Don Pedro said so or not he'd be bound to feel that in some way we'd been responsible, particularly if he knew I'd given money to José for drink.'

Bertie got up. 'Okay, old boy. I'll press on. If I don't meet you on the track I'll see you back here.'

'If the *Intendente* doesn't want me for anything I'll snatch an early lunch and come along. That'll give you a chance to come back for something to eat.'

'Fair enough.' Bertie departed on his errand.

Biggles waited in the bar until the police officer re-appeared. They had a drink together at the bar. Nothing was said about Dolores, the arrest of Maria, or the affair at the Casa Floresta, and after a little while the party broke up.

Biggles went out into the yard, and afterwards took a walk round the town hoping to catch sight of José. He saw no sign of him. Puzzled, for the Negro's pony was still there he returned to the hotel, and after a wash went into the dining room for lunch.

CHAPTER 11

BERTIE
MAKES A BLUNDER

BERTIE went with confidence about his task of watching for Neckel to make a move at the Casa Floresta, for with ample cover available it appeared to offer no difficulty, particularly as Neckel's coloured bodyguard had been killed and there could hardly have been time to replace him. It was not until he was near the house, making a cautious approach, that he realised it might not be as easy as he had imagined. It was not that there was any shortage of cover. There was too much.

It would have been a simple matter to watch the track from somewhere near the fork; but while this was the way Neckel would probably take should he decide to vacate the house, there was no certainty of it. To make sure he did not slip away unobserved it would be necessary to watch both doors, and the river, in case Neckel had by some means been able to get another canoe. That was a possibility not to be ignored. He might have asked the *Intendente,* who knew he had lost his boat, to send another one down from the town by water. The question arose, therefore, which was the best position to keep such a watch that it would be impossible for Neckel to get away without being seen?

After a short reconnaissance he decided the ideal place

would be from somewhere nearer the river, and he settled on a spot which, from where he stood, he thought commanded a view both of the water and the open front of the house. He would be able to see the front door clearly, and the path that led to the courtyard where he knew there was a second door. He had seen Neckel use it on the occasion of his previous visit, the night when Maria had burst in on Neckel and Dolores.

To reach the place he had in mind meant leaving the track, and it was only when he set out to get to it that he discovered the difficulties of trying to find a passage through virgin jungle. It was not merely a matter of picking a way. It was necessary to force a way, and in places cut a path through the lush tropical growth. However, he resolved to go on with it; but he was soon in difficulties. The giant trees seemed to reach to the sky. Everywhere lianas coiled in a fantastic tangle of loops as they climbed endlessly towards the sunlight, clutching at anything for support. Vines sprang from tree to tree in their desperate efforts to reach the same objective. They rose from the ground at all angles, in and out and over the roots of trees which, like the legs of monstrous beasts, spread everywhere. Some had air roots hanging from their branches, like long bunches of whip thongs. The ground was a swamp and he was often up to the knees in slush. The heat was suffocating. The stench of rotting vegetable matter nearly choked him, and all the time he was the centre of a cloud of voracious insects. Once, taking hold of a branch to steady himself, without noticing that it was perforated with small holes, he gasped when he discovered it was, or seemed to be, red hot. From every hole came pouring a stream of little red ants, biting or stinging unmercifully as they ran over his hand. It took him a minute or two to knock them off. Even then the burning of the stings remained.

Bertie realised he had made a mistake in leaving the track, but having come so far with so much trouble he resolved to go on. He didn't like being beaten and he thought he hadn't much farther to go. Peering ahead he could see the river, which suggested the forest became a little more open. He would at least have no trouble in finding his way back, for he had left a track that might have been made by an elephant. Pausing for breath he could understand why Don Pedro had given up orchid hunting personally. It was not surprising that wild orchids were expensive.

As he stood there he heard a noise of crashing undergrowth that made it clear he was not alone in the forest. Was it a man or an animal? Climbing on a root he was just in time to see the back of a Negro, nearer the river, just disappearing behind a growth of tall ferns. Who or what the man was doing there he couldn't imagine. Nor did he care. Such was his state of heat and exasperation that he thought no more about him; for now that he was near the place for which he had been making he saw that all his efforts had been in vain. All he could see was the roof of the house, for a belt of bamboo intervened. Angry with himself for his folly, which had resulted in so much labour and loss of time, he decided he would do better to go back to the track after all. From where he stood he could see practically nothing.

Turning to retrace his steps he became aware of a

curious sound close at hand. Actually, he had heard it before, but then it had been farther away. He had taken it to be the hissing chatter of an angry monkey, of which there were plenty in the trees. Now he was not so sure. What was a monkey doing on the ground, anyway, and so close to him? Lowering his eyes to the direction from which the strange noise was approaching, more from curiosity than alarm, he tracked it down to some ferns, a few feet away.

What he saw froze him in his tracks, his nerves quivering from shock. A pair of eyes were fixed on his own in a glassy stare. Below them a slender tongue slithered in and out of a horrible mouth like a piece of automatic machinery. Under the head was a huge body, coil upon coil of snake as thick as his thigh. He knew from its size that it could only be an anaconda.

It is claimed by some travellers that the anaconda, for all its huge dimensions, is not a dangerous reptile, saying that if disturbed it will usually try only to escape. Others hold a different view, notably natives who often come in contact with it. It certainly is not venomous. It kills by constriction and swallows its prey hole, as do other snakes, boa constrictors and pythons, of similar size. Bertie, who may have disturbed the creature, was now able to judge for himself.

He saw the snake's head being drawn back. Very slowly. The top coil of its long body became shaped like a letter 'S'. He had seen snakes before and he knew it was going to strike; yet before he could move, the head had shot forward, the body unwinding like a spring. He just had time to bend sideways, at the same time throw-

ing up an arm to protect his face. This served its purpose, but the backward-sloping teeth became caught up
in the loose sleeve of his shirt. Instinctively he gave his
arm a vicious jerk to free it, and in this he succeeded at
the cost of losing much of his shirt, which remained in
the creature's mouth, hanging from the teeth.

He would now have run, had this been possible. It
was not. In fact, he could hardly move at all. One foot
seemed anchored to the ground. Looking down he saw
the reason. The snake had its tail coiled round his leg.
On falling after its strike it had not turned, but with its
enormous body extending to a fantastic length it began
to move towards the river. In a moment he was being
dragged along with it, and it was only with the greatest
difficulty that he was able to keep on his feet. Vines
were pulled across his face.

It is in moments of extreme peril that the human
brain is at its best. Bertie did not panic. He did not have
to think. His head was perfectly clear. He could see
everything distinctly, and realised the snake was trying
to get him to the water. He reached for his machete and
whipped it from its sheath. Swinging it, he brought the
heavy blade down with all his strength across the tail
within inches of his leg. The knife sliced through it. The
snake's body seemed to shiver. With the two severed
ends oozing blood it let out a hiss like the safety valve of
a locomotive. But it went on, leaving its tail, about a
yard of it, squirming about in the trampled herbage.

Bertie did not stay to watch what became of the body.
He was on his way out of the jungle regardless of obstacles which in ordinary circumstances would have

T—E

stopped him. It was during this rush to the track, as he realised presently, that he did himself more mischief than the snake had done, although his wounds were no more than bruises and scratches.

Reaching the track, after making sure there was no one in sight, he crossed over to the far side and sank wearily into a convenient growth of ferns. With hands still shaking from shock he mopped his face and neck with his handkerchief, for he was sweating, as the saying is, from every pore. This done he examined the worst of his scratches and his torn clothes. There was nothing he could do about the missing sleeve of his shirt, and was only thankful that the material had been flimsy enough to tear. After that he moved back a little way, to a place where he could not be seen from the track, and settled down with his chin in his hands to recover his composure.

For half an hour all remained quiet, by which time he was more or less back to normal. The sound of footsteps approaching from the direction of the town brought him to the alert, and risking a peep he saw to his great relief that it was Biggles. As Biggles drew level he showed himself.

Biggles stared at him. 'What on earth have you been doing to yourself?'

Bertie smiled weakly. 'Matter of fact, old boy, I've just had a bit of an argument with an anaconda.'

'You seem to have got the worst of it.'

'No fear. The brute's gone home without his tail. You never saw such a monster in your life. He was as long as Regent Street.'

'*How* long?'

'Well, there must have been fifty feet of him.'

'How big was he – really?'

'I'll swear he was over twenty feet.'*

'That's better. How did it happen?'

Bertie described his adventure in detail, first having explained his reason for going into the forest. 'You can ask me to do anything you like,' he concluded, 'but I'm not doing any more jungling. If I hadn't had a machete I should have been up the creek without a paddle.'

'Have you seen anyone?'

'Not a soul. No, that isn't quite true,' corrected Bertie, remembering the Negro he had seen in the forest. 'For a moment I did catch sight of a Negro among the trees, but I've no idea who he was. I don't think he saw me. Come to think of it, he may have been the bloke who flushed that beastly snake.'

'You're all right now?'

'Right as rain.'

'Fine. In that case I'll take over while you go back to the pub for something to eat.'

'Do you want me to come back here?'

'You might as well, if you feel up to it. There's nothing doing at the hotel. Together we might try

---

* The size an anaconda, which is a water snake, can reach, still provides a subject for argument. It is generally thought that thirty feet is about the outside limit, twenty feet being nearer normal. But there are travellers who claim to have seen specimens up to forty feet, while Indians claim they can grow larger than that. The anaconda rests in or near water, and will usually try to drag its prey into it.

getting a bit closer to the house. One can keep watch while the other explores.'

'Good idea. Did you see anything of José?'

'Not a sign. His pony is still in the stable, so you'll probably find him in the bar when you get back. If he's still drinking you might try to stop him. Threaten to tell Don Pedro if he doesn't pack up.'

'I'll do that.'

'Just one last thing. I'm worried about Bogosoff. He's got a gun, and he doesn't clutter himself up with hardware for nothing. Notice the way he or his pal shot Neckel's bodyguard out of hand. What I feel is this. If we get into an argument with him he'll have the drop on us. I'd feel happier with a gun in my pocket. You'll find my pocket automatic and a couple of clips of cartridges wrapped in a shirt at the bottom of my kitbag. Slip a clip in the pistol and put it in your pocket when you come back.'

'Good enough. Believe you me, I wished I had a gun in my pocket when I saw that anaconda giving me a dirty look. This is no place for kid gloves.'

'I couldn't agree more. That's all. Push along and get some grub.'

'I'm ready for it. See you later.' Bertie departed.

Seeing nothing of interest he did not stop until he reached the hotel, where he made straight for the bar. José was not there so he went out to the yard. Not seeing him there he spoke to the stable-boy, from whom, to his surprise, he learned that José, taking his pony, had returned to the Villa Vanda.

'How long ago was this?'

'About half an hour, *señor*.'

Greatly puzzled that the Negro should go off without saying good-bye, and wondering where he could have spent the morning. Bertie went back into the hotel and had a long overdue meal.

CHAPTER 12

FRUSTRATED

IT was late afternoon, with the heat of the day past and the sun going down in a blaze of golden light, when Bertie rejoined Biggles on the track through the primeval forest. Like many roads, no doubt it had originally been a path made through the ages by generations of wild animals going down to the river to drink.

'Anything doing?' he asked.

'Not a thing.'

'You haven't seen anyone?'

'Not a soul. And there hasn't been a sound from the house.'

'Have you been any closer to it?'

'Yes. I've twice been as near as I dare without risk of being seen. The place might have been abandoned for any signs of life I've heard. I'm getting a bit worried about it. We'd feel silly if, after having spent so much time here, we learned that Neckel was already miles away. But short of going and knocking on the door it's hard to see what we can do about it.'

'How about having another look round?'

'Now you're here we might move a little nearer. If there's anyone there, sooner or later we should see or hear him moving about. We shall know for certain if

anyone is at home when it gets dark, which won't be long.
At least, I can't imagine anyone sitting in the house
without a light. Let's go on. Keep your eyes skinned.'

'You needn't tell me to do that. After my affair with
the anaconda I'm watching where I put my feet. These
jungles aren't what they're cracked up to be. Fotherham
can have all the orchids.'

Keeping a sharp look-out and listening after every
few steps, they went on slowly until they were in a position to see the front door. It was shut. There was no one
in sight. Moving on again Bertie led the way to the place
from where he had watched the scene, in the little courtyard, between Neckel, Dolores and Maria. There was
no one there, either. Nor was there a sound.

'There must be somebody in the place,' said Bertie.
'That side door's open.'

'Then let's watch for a bit. It doesn't seem likely that
Neckel would go out leaving his door open.'

'They watched for perhaps half an hour. The sun set.
Darkness closed in with tropical swiftness. Fireflies appeared. Crickets chirped. Frogs croaked. The mosquitoes attacked in hordes. But no light appeared at any
window of the silent house.

'I don't get it,' muttered Biggles. 'There's something
wrong here. It looks now as if Neckel must have pulled
out.'

'How about taking the bull by the horns?'

'How?'

'By going to the door and knocking.'

'We'd better wait a bit longer before we go as far as
that. It's possible that Neckel has only gone out for

some reason and may come back at any moment. I'd rather he didn't find us in the house. He knows that Bogosoff is after those papers, but he has had no reason to suppose we're here for the same purpose.'

More time passed. A full moon soared up over the river to splash the ripples with lines of quicksilver. It all looked very peaceful and beautiful. Only the house, with palm fronds throwing a weird pattern of black shadows on its white face, seemed to have surrounded itself in an atmosphere of mystery.

'I've had enough of this,' said Biggles at last. 'We can't stay here all night being torn to pieces by these infernal mosquitoes. I'm going over to that side door. If there's anyone the other side of it he would have closed it by now instead of leaving it open for all the bugs under creation to wander in.' As he finished speaking he strode purposefully to the door.

Reaching it he stopped. Inside all was in darkness. Not a sound.

'Let's go in,' decided Biggles. 'This may be our chance to look for the papers. We'll try the sitting room first. If Neckel suddenly shows up it'll be just too bad; but we'll tackle that situation should it arise. What a fool I was not to bring a torch. Have you got any matches on you? I've only got my lighter.'

Bertie produced a box.

'Good. We should be able to find a candle, a lamp, or something.' Biggles struck a match. Its light revealed a short corridor with a door at the end. It stood ajar. There was no light inside the room except that provided by the moon, which showed as a pale strip the length of the door. 'I fancy that's the sitting room,' he whispered, as the match burnt itself out.

He went on to the door and with the greatest possible caution pushed it open.

No more matches were necessary, for the room was flooded with blue moonlight pouring through the window. He took stock of it. He listened. 'There can't be anyone in the house,' he asserted. 'Let's get busy and find those papers.'

'If they're still here.'

'You've said something. If Neckel's gone the chances are he's taken them with him. I see a lamp on the table. We might as well light it to see better what we're up to. I've no compunction about what we're doing. Neckel's a thief, anyway, so if he finds us here he'll have nothing to shout about.'

Biggles advanced towards the lamp, but after taking two or three paces he stumbled over something on the floor. Looking down he caught his breath sharply.

'What is it?' asked Bertie, quickly.

'There's somebody here. On the floor. Stand fast while I light the lamp.'

This was done, and the moonbeams were banished by yellow lamplight. For a few seconds neither Biggles nor Bertie spoke. With horror on their faces they could only stare at what lay at their feet. It was a body: the head in a pool of blood. The throat had been slashed. It was Neckel.

'My God!' breathed Biggles. 'What a mess.'

Bertie said nothing.

'I thought there was something fishy about the place,

but I wasn't expecting anything like this,' went on Biggles, tersely.

'The sooner we're out of here the better,' rejoined Bertie. 'If we're found with this on the floor we shall have some explaining to do. Who on earth could have done it?'

'I don't know and I don't care.'

'Bogosoff?'

'No. Bogosoff would have used a gun. This was the work of a knife, probably a machete. Moreover, had Bogosoff been here it would have been to search for the papers, in which case we'd see signs of the place having been ransacked. As far as I can see nothing has been touched.'

A strange expression came into Bertie's eyes. 'I'll tell you who did it.'

'Who?'

'José'

'Never.'

'Why not? He spent the morning swilling *aguardiente* and had worked himself into a mood for any devilment. He was handy with a machete. Remember, he held Neckel, or Salvador as he called him, responsible for Dolores' death. If he did this he wouldn't walk back to the town along the track for fear of meeting someone who knew him. He'd keep out of sight. I told you I'd seen a coloured man in the forest. If I'm right it would explain why José suddenly decided to go home in such a hurry.'

Biggles bit his lip. 'I'm afraid you're right on the beam. It certainly adds up, the way you've put it. Pity.

But never mind about that now we've no time to lose. I'm not going without the papers if they're here. Open the front door and warn me if you see anyone coming. With both doors open we shall have an escape route if we're disturbed. Don't go far away, though.'

'I get it.' Bertie went through to the front of the house.

Biggles went over to the picture, an unglazed oil painting of a religious subject, in a deep gilt frame, measuring about two feet by eighteen inches, behind which he thought the papers might have been hidden. He lifted the cord off its hook. Disappointment awaited him. The wall behind it was bare. He put the picture on a nearby side table, and returning to the place where it had been he pushed and prodded hoping to locate a secret spring. Nothing happened. He stood back dismayed when he realised that this meant the entire house might have to be searched, which would take a long time. But there was nothing else for it. If he was to recover the missing documents it was now or never, for once the police took over, as no doubt they would when they learned what had happened to the tenant, it would be more difficult than ever to gain access to the house.

There was an antique Spanish writing-desk against the wall under the place where the picture had hung. It seemed as good a place as any to start so he opened it and started going through the compartments inside. Five minutes' work established that the papers, which he imagined would be in a large envelope or tied together, were not there.

There were four drawers down the side of the desk.

He pulled out the top one. Suddenly he stopped, tense. He had not heard a sound; but by instinct or intuition a feeling had come over him that he was not alone in the room; that he was being watched. The fact that his nerves were keyed up may have been responsible. He spun round.

Just inside the door by which he had entered the room stood Bogosoff, covering him with a gun.

'Carry on,' said Bogosoff, smoothly, with a cynical smile. 'You're saving me a lot of trouble.'

Biggles' jaw set. What was Bertie doing to allow this to happen? Had Bogosoff been in the house all the time? were the thoughts that flashed through his brain. No matter. All that mattered was, the man was there. He must have seen the light and knew where to come.

'What do you think you're doing?' said Biggles, shortly, really to gain time to recover from shock. He spoke loudly, hoping Bertie would hear his voice.

'Surely that question is quite unnecessary,' sneered Bogosoff.

'You see what's on the floor.'

'Of course. If you had to kill that miserable traitor you needn't have made such a mess.'

'I didn't kill him.'

'What does it matter? I would have killed him, anyhow. I shall also kill you without the slightest hesitation if you don't do exactly as I tell you. I have no personal grudge against you, but business is business. Stand with your back to the wall.' Bogosoff indicated the place with the muzzle of his pistol.

Biggles obeyed. Caught at a disadvantage this was not

the moment to open active resistance. That could come
later. Bertie was outside. He could only hope he
wouldn't walk into the room unprepared and get himself shot. At present it was obvious from the way
Bogosoff was behaving that he was unaware of Bertie's
proximity. But the overwhelming fact in Biggles' mind
was that Bogosoff had not yet got the papers, or he
wouldn't be there. It was a relief to know that.

With his eyes on Biggles Bogosoff advanced to the
desk. 'Don't try anything foolish,' he advised. 'I'm not
carrying this gun as a decoration. If the papers are not in
this room I shall have to try the others, in which case
you will be in my way. To avoid the unpleasant consequences of that I'll make you a proposition. If you will
give me your solemn word of honour to go away and not
return I'll allow you to go.'

Biggles could see Bogosoff's difficulty. The man could
hardly search the house, going from room to room in the
dark, taking him with him. He wouldn't be able to
search and watch him at the same time.

'I'm giving you nothing,' he said coldly.

'As you wish. But be very careful.'

Biggles took care not to move or show any emotion
when a movement at the far door caught his eye and he
saw Bertie standing there, gun in hand. Apparently he
had either seen Bogosoff arrive and had followed him in,
or hearing voices had come to investigate. His eyes,
seeing that Biggles had noticed him, asked a question.

Rather than speak or make a signal to Bertie Biggles
decided to take the initiative. For one thing he realised
that Bertie would not dare to use his gun for fear of

hitting him because he was standing directly in line with Bogosoff.

'You've got it all wrong,' he told Bogosoff. 'Do you suppose I'd be such a fool as to come here alone?'

Bogosoff took no notice. Standing sideways to the desk so that he could keep one eye on Biggles, he started throwing out the contents of the drawers.

'I'm telling you,' went on Biggles. 'Take a look behind you.'

Bogosoff smiled sourly. 'Try something a little more original.'

Bertie stepped in. 'Drop that gun,' he said crisply.

Hearing the voice behind him Bogosoff whipped round, half raising the gun.

Biggles took a swift pace forward and snatching up the picture from the table brought the heavy frame crashing down on Bogosoff's head. The man did not fall, but he staggered under the blow, dropping the gun as his hands went to where he had been struck. Tossing the picture back on the table, Biggles kicked the pistol clear and picked it up.

'Now I'll give the orders,' he rapped out.

The position was now reversed. It was Bogosoff who was going to be in the way when they proceeded to search the house. He saw a way out of the difficulty.

'Bertie, you might cut the cord off that picture and use it to tie Mr Bogosoff's hands while we get on with this daft business,' he requested.

Bertie cut the cord with his penknife and tied Bogosoff's hands behind his back while Biggles kept him covered. This done Biggles pushed him into an easy

chair, saying: 'Now it's your turn to keep still. Keep an
eye on him Bertie while I get on with the job.'

The job, of course, was to make a thorough search for
the missing documents.

To ransack a house for one particular object, and a
small one at that, is not an easy task in any conditions: in
the peculiar circumstances, what with the darkness and
the fact that Biggles did not know his way about, it was
clear to him from the outset that the operation was
going to take time; probably a lot of time. To make
things more difficult it was not absolutely certain that
the papers were there.

First he finished the room they were in. Then he went
to what was clearly Neckel's bedroom. Not finding there
what he sought, he went through the rest of the house. It
was all to no purpose. He was disappointed, but he was
not surprised. Not from the start had he expected to find
the papers in an obvious place. They would be hidden,
and Neckel would give some thought to the matter. It
was more than an hour later when Biggles returned to
the sitting-room where Bertie was still standing guard
over the prisoner. As a final hope, a remote one, he went
through Neckel's pockets.

'No use,' he said moodily, as he rose from this grue-
some performance. He looked at Bogosoff, who was
smiling cynically. 'It looks as if we've both been wasting
our time.' He turned back to Bertie. 'Well, we can't stay
here all night. Now we've got his gun, and as we can't
take him with us, we might as well let our friend go.'

Bogosoff continued to smile.

Bertie removed the cord from his wrists.

Bogosoff stood up, rubbing them.

'Clear out and stay out,' ordered Biggles, frostily.

The man went without a word.

Biggles lit a cigarette. 'This looks like being the end of the trail,' he remarked lugubriously. 'There's only one thing left for us to do. If those papers are in this house, if we can't get them I'll see that no one else does.'

'How are you going to manage that?'

'I'm going to set fire to the house.'

Bertie started. '*What* did you say?'

'You heard me. My orders were, if I couldn't get the papers I was to take any steps to see that no one else gets them. That's plain enough. Bear in mind if these papers got into the wrong hands they could start a war. They may not be here. If they are somewhere else, with Neckel dead they're likely to remain where they are indefinitely. If they *are* here, should Bogosoff come back he can amuse himself going through the ashes.'

Bertie looked shocked. 'But I say, old boy, that's a bit steep.'

'It'll be steeper if someone else finds those papers and realises their importance,' returned Biggles grimly.

'But what about him?' Bertie indicated the dead man.

'He's past caring what happens. If cremation was good enough for the Roman emperors it should be good enough for him.' Biggles spoke in a voice bitter with frustration.

'And having done that, what next?'

'We go home. And I'm not stopping to pick orchids.'

'What are you going to tell the police.'

'Nothing. I shan't say a word about us having been here. When I get back to headquarters I want to be able to tell the chief that I have good reason for thinking the papers no longer exist.'

'Then you still think they may be somewhere in this house?'

'They could be. It's the most likely place. I must have been an optimist to suppose Neckel would put them where they could easily be found. He must have known an attempt would be made to recover them and he'd take steps accordingly. To get at them, if they're here, could mean taking the house down brick by brick.'

'Before we send the place up in flames don't you think it would be better to leave things as they are and come back in daylight, when we'd be better able to see what we're doing, for a final check.'

'We'd probably find the police here.'

'Not if we came early. It might be some time before Neckel's body is discovered. At a pinch you might take the *Intendente* into your confidence. Tell him the whole story. He's well disposed towards us. Moreover he's a pal of Don Pedro. If it comes to that we could ride out to the Villa Vanda and ask Don Pedro to put in a word for us. I'm sure he'd do anything to help. He should know from experience how to handle the police. He's no fool. He must know jolly well that we didn't really come out here to pick posies.'

Biggles considered the suggestion. 'Perhaps you're right,' he conceded. 'When I talked of setting fire to the place I was pretty well at my wits' end. Here we are, in the house. We've done pretty well to get as far as this, but I'm afraid it's as far as we can go. We still haven't got what we came for. What a spot to be in.'

'We'd better make up our minds.'

Biggles reached a decision. 'I'll tell you what we'll do. We'll go back to the hotel and try to grab a few hours' sleep. At the crack of dawn we'll ride out here on the ponies. If there's no one here we'll make a final search. If the police are here we'll ride straight on to the Villa Vanda, without going back to the town, and tell Don Pedro all about it. I'll ask for his advice.'

Bertie nodded. 'I'm with you. It's about all we can do.'

'Then let's get on with it.'

Having put out the lamp they left the house, closing the doors behind them.

CHAPTER 13

ONE LAST CHANCE

THE stars were one by one dying in the sky before the advance of the mounting sun when, the following morning, Biggles and Bertie went out into the yard and having saddled their ponies set off in the direction of the Casa Floresta for what they expected would be for the last time – as in fact it was. Biggles was in a sombre mood, for as he had said, if they failed to find the missing documents it would mean returning home to report failure, or near failure. With Neckel dead their one contact with the papers had disappeared, and only time would show whether or not they had passed into the possession of someone else.

What the *patron* of the hotel must be thinking of their strange behaviour Biggles neither knew nor cared. The gloves were off and he was prepared to do anything, go to any lengths to bring his mission to a successful conclusion, if that were possible, regardless of what anyone might think.

Bertie took a more philosophical view. They had done everything humanly possible and no one could do more than that, he asserted.

When, in the grey light of the new day, with clouds of tenuous mist rising like steam from the valleys, they reached the house of death, they found it silent and apparently deserted. The doors were still closed. Taking the horses into some convenient trees, they tethered them and continued on foot. Biggles wasted no time on preliminary scouting. He went straight to the front door. Without knocking he opened it and with Bertie close behind walked into the sitting-room. At first sight everything appeared to be precisely as they had last seen it. Neckel's body still lay on the floor.

Suddenly Biggles stiffened. 'Somebody has been here since last night,' he said in a thin, brittle voice.

'How do you know?'

'Look at that picture! The one I took off the wall. After I'd hit Bogosoff on the head with it I threw it on that table. It was still in one piece. Now look at it. Pulled to pieces and half of it on the floor.'

Bertie looked. The heavy gilt frame was there. So was the canvas, although it had a large hole in it. But the thin backing boards lay in strips and splinters on the carpet, as if someone had tried to make matchwood of them. 'How very odd,' he said. 'Why should anyone do a thing like that?'

Biggles went on in a curiously calm voice. 'Don't you realise what has happened?'

'No, I'm dashed if I do.'

With such an expression on his face as Bertie had never seen there before Biggles murmured, still quite calmly: 'We've made the biggest boob we ever made in our lives. It's all as plain as a pikestaff. I was right about that picture. The papers must have been between the backing and the canvas. I may have split the backing when I cracked Bogosoff on the skull and so exposed them. I never looked at the thing again. It's the only possible answer. No one but a raving lunatic would come in here and, with a dead man on the floor, start to tear a picture to pieces for no reason whatsoever.'

Bertie clapped a hand to his head. 'Imagine it! The papers were right here under our noses all the time. Now someone else has found them.'

'Not someone. Bogosoff. Who else would be likely to come here? Who else could know about the papers? Last night he waited for us to go; then he came back to make another search. I realised that might happen, but what else could we do other than let him go? We couldn't shoot him in cold blood; nor could we take him back to the town with us. Anyhow, as I hadn't been able to find the papers I thought it long odds against him finding them if he did come back. Why should he go near that picture? Well, your guess is as good as mine. He may be interested in painting. He may have wondered why it had been taken down. I may have split that flimsy backing when I hit him and so exposed something white inside. But never mind how it happened. Let's face it, it's a million to one he's away with the papers. That's why he isn't here. It's time I had my head examined. When I get home I'll hand in my resignation.'

'No use going on like that, old boy,' protested Bertie. 'There was no reason for you to look twice at the picture. Bogosoff can't have got far.'

'Far enough.'

'Not if he had the same idea as we had, and waited for daylight before he came back.'

'Without knowing which way he's gone it isn't much use looking for him.'

'He didn't go towards the town or we'd have met him. I can't imagine him leaving the track.'

'That's true.' Biggles frowned. 'Just a minute. I've remembered something; something Don Pedro said when we arrived at his place and I suggested going on to Cruzuado by the river. He said it wasn't possible while the river was in flood. Even the steamboat service couldn't get beyond – what did he call the place – Puerto Vecho, about twenty miles downstream. The river's still running high and strong, so the conditions are the same.'

'And so?'

'Don Pedro said that as a result, the Russian he had spoken to, who had just arrived, had had to disembark at Puerto Vecho and finish his journey overland. I remember seeing this place Puerto Vecho as we flew up the river. Boiled down it means that if Bogosoff didn't use the track, or tramp through the jungle, he must have come here by water.'

'I don't quite see what you're getting at.'

'All right. Bogosoff didn't leave here by the track or we would have seen him. Right?'

'Right.'

'Then short of hacking a path through the jungle he must have left by the river. Right?'

'Right?'

'That means he must have come here by the river.'

'Right. But how?'

'By canoe. He'd got one. Neckel kept one here presumably in case he wanted to get away in a hurry. Bogosoff pinched it. I saw him.'

'Ah yes. Now I'm with you. Bogosoff must have parked the canoe somewhere and used it to come back. Now he's gone off in it.'

'What more likely? He isn't here. If he left here in a canoe there's only one way he could have gone, and that's downstream. Don Pedro told us it was almost impossible to get upstream with the river in this state. Not even the steamboat could make headway against the stream. So if he's on the river he's going down, probably making for Puerto Vecho, where he'd be able to board a steamer returning to Manaos.'

'He might have crossed the river to the other side, to Brazil.'

'I doubt it. There's nothing there except jungle. He'd never get straight across anyway. He'd be swept downstream, and if he landed he'd be faced with miles of walking through sheer jungle, and you know what that's like. I can't see him doing that. I'd say he's heading down the river, making for the first settlement where transport is available, and that's Puerto Vecho.'

'If he left here in daylight he couldn't have got there yet.'

'That's how I see it. It's twenty miles, and even with the river running as fast as it is I can't see him getting there in less than a couple of hours. Reckoning he must be safe from pursuit, he'll see no reason to take chances by being in too much of a hurry. In the aircraft we could cover the whole length of the river in a matter of minutes.'

'We've got to get to it.'

'We've got horses.'

'If Bogosoff's pal is still with him, wearing that white bush jacket, we should be able to spot it a mile away.'

'It's a chance. Let's go.'

'What will you do if we do spot him?'

'I'll decide that if and when the time comes. Let's get cracking.'

They ran to the horses.

The ride that followed was something neither of them was ever likely to forget. When they had covered the same ground before, with José leading a packhorse, immediately after the rain in the heavy going, they had travelled at a walk. Bertie hadn't checked the time for the journey, but he thought it had taken not less than two hours. Now, constantly urging their mounts to the best speed possible, they did it under the hour. They had this advantage. As a result of the fine weather the ground had largely dried out, and there were one or two places where it was possible to proceed at a canter. And, of course, there was no packhorse to lead. The heat was formidable, and both men and horses streamed perspiration. The usual cloud of flies and other insects were a tribulation that had to be endured.

When they arrived at the Villa they saw Don Pedro in the yard with José and some of his orchid collectors. They all stared in astonishment as Biggles sprang from his pony and, without stopping to unsaddle, ran on to the little pier where the Gadfly was moored.

Bertie shouted: 'Sorry. Can't stop now. We'll be

back,' and leaving José to unsaddle their sweating ponies raced on after Biggles.

Not a word was spoken as, having cast off, they scrambled into their seats in the cockpit. Without troubling to fasten the safety belt Biggles reached for the starter. A minute was lost getting the engines going, but as soon as they came to life they had a chance to warm up as the aircraft surged towards the open river. Without waiting to check anything, for every second was precious, Biggles took off, risking collision with floating debris. Airborne, Bertie breathed again. 'Don Pedro will think we've gone raving mad,' he remarked.

'And he won't be far wrong,' answered Biggles.

Holding the machine low he headed downstream, feeling sure that if Bogosoff was on the water he would by this time be well below them. 'Keep your eyes open for a canoe with one or two people in it,' he shouted. 'For a start I'll keep close to this bank.' By this he meant the side of the river on which the Casa Floresta was situated.

With the river at this point getting on for half a mile wide there was plenty of water to watch, but owing to the flood there was little traffic on it, and, as was to be expected, it was all going downstream. For the most part such craft as they saw were on the big side, either *batelones*, huge canoes with palm-thatched roofs such as Don Pedro used for transporting his bulbs to Manaos or *callapos*, which are several balsa rafts fastened together. Ordinary small canoes were few and far between, and close investigation invariably showed them to be primitive dug-outs with a single native occupant.

Rounding a bend Puerto Vecho came into sight without them having seen the craft they sought.

'I'll go back up the other side,' said Biggles. 'That canoe is on the river somewhere.'

He was right. It was. Within five minutes a spot of white caught Bertie's eyes, and concentrating on it he made it out to be the jacket of one of two people in a canoe which must have been travelling close to the opposite bank. It was now cutting diagonally across the stream as if making for Puerto Vecho. He called Biggles' attention to it.

'That's 'em,' confirmed Bertie tersely, as the aircraft flew low over the canoe, deep in the water under its double load.

What Biggles had decided to do should the circumstance arise he didn't know. Nothing more had been said about it. He was soon to know.

'I'm going to have those papers or they can go to the bottom of the Rio Jurara,' announced Biggles grimly.

Bringing the machine round in a steep bank he roared over the canoe at a height of not more than a few feet. If the purpose of this was to throw the occupants into a panic it succeeded. Apparently thinking they were about to be rammed they ducked in such haste that the canoe nearly went over. It shipped a fair amount of water before it recovered. Turning again Biggles made a landing which ended within a score of yards of the objective. A burst of throttle took the machine on as close as it was possible to get, the hull nearly touching the canoe.

Opening his side window Biggles shouted: 'Hand over those papers or I'll sink you.'

Bogosoff's answer was to push the canoe clear with a paddle and resume paddling.

'All right. You've asked for it,' yelled Biggles.

He taxied to a distance of perhaps fifty yards, swung round, and then bore down at speed on the canoe as if he really did intend to ram it. He nearly did, by accident, for this was something he would not have dared to risk. When the machine was within yards of the canoe a long black object rose out of the water dead in line with them, and to his horror Bertie saw it was the branch of a big tree, turning over as it rolled down on the flood. 'Look out,' he cried.

But Biggles had also seen the tree, and did the only thing possible if they were to avoid a collision with an object solid and heavy enough to rip a hole in the keel. He swerved, yawing so violently that the port wing tip touched the water, causing the machine to swing directly towards the canoe. The hull missed it by inches, but the effect on the canoe was much the same. Struck first by the bow wave and then the wash of the wake it filled with water and capsized, leaving the two occupants clinging to it with only their arms and head showing above water.

Again Biggles brought the machine round and ended up alongside the upside-down canoe. 'Take over,' he told Bertie, and leaving his seat hurried aft to the cabin. He opened the door to find himself a yard from Bogosoff. The man's face was ghastly, as it had cause to be, for Amazonian rivers have some exceptionally nasty inhabitants that appear always to be hungry. Apart from alligators there are the voracious razor-toothed piranhas which travel in shoals and will tear a man to pieces in minutes, and the *tembladores*, the electric eels which Don Pedro had mentioned.

'Give me those documents and I'll take you to the bank,' said Biggles quickly, for both craft were fast being carried down the river.

This time Bogosoff did not argue. Putting a hand in a breast pocket he pulled out a long black wallet with a zip fastener. Biggles snatched it out of his hand and opened it to glance at the contents to make sure he was not being fooled. Satisfied, he put the wallet in his pocket, helped Bogosoff and his companion, streaming water, to get on board and called Bertie.

'Keep an eye on these two,' he ordered curtly. 'I'm running them over to the bank.' So saying he went forward to the controls and taxied to a muddy beach at the bend just above Puerto Vecho. He called to Bertie: 'Okay. Get 'em ashore.'

The two men stepped out into the mud and splashed their way to higher ground.

Biggles took the machine clear, and in a minute or two it was in the air heading upstream towards the Villa Vanda.

When they had landed and taxied in Don Pedro came down to the pier to meet them.

'I'm terribly sorry about that,' said Biggles apologetically, as he made fast. 'It was rude of us, but I hadn't time to explain. If you'll be kind enough to give us a drink I'll tell you what it was all about. We owe you that after your help and hospitality.'

Presently, in the house, with some refreshments before them, he did that.

'And what are you going to do now?' asked Don Pedro, when he had finished.

'Get back home as quickly as possible to set a few minds at rest. But before I do that we shall have to go to Cruzuado to collect our kit and pay the hotel bill.'

'I can do that for you,' offered Don Pedro. 'There's no need for you to go. You both look as if you could do with a wash and brush up. If you like I'll send José into the town to collect your gear. At the same time he can tell the *patron* I'll be along myself in a day or two to settle up. You wait here. It'll give you a chance to have a square meal before you start.'

'Thank you. That's a kind offer I shall not decline,' accepted Biggles, gratefully. 'I don't mind admitting that after the rate we've been going for the past few days I could do with a breather.'

'That goes for me, too,' put in Bertie. 'After the flap we've had this morning I'm still not sure whether we're coming or going.'

And so it was settled. When a few hours later they thanked their host and said good-bye to José they had still said no word about the finding of the body in the Casa Floresta. Biggles thought it better that José should not know they suspected him of the murder. As he said, it was only suspicion. They had no proof, and as far as he was concerned, as José had served them well he'd rather not know the truth.

*   *   *

Five days later Biggles walked into his chief's office at Scotland Yard and laid the wallet on his desk. 'I think that's what you wanted, sir.'

The Air Commodore sprang to his feet. 'You mean you've got those papers!' he exclaimed. 'I can't believe it.'

'Neither can I,' returned Biggles, dryly. 'You'd better have a look.'

The Air Commodore opened the wallet and examined the contents. Having done so he drew a breath of relief that seemed to come from his heart. 'Yes, these are the ones,' he confirmed. 'What's happened to them? They're all cockled, as if they'd been wet.'

'I'm not surprised. I feel a bit cockled myself. At one moment they were within inches of going to the bottom of the Rio Jurara.'

'How did that happen?'

'It's rather a long story, sir. Knowing you'd be anxious, I came straight here before going home to change. If you'll give me a little while to get straightened out I'll tell you all about it.' Biggles smiled wanly. 'Sorry I hadn't time to pick you a bunch of orchids.'

The Air Commodore returned the papers to the wallet. 'These are all the flowers I wanted.'

'Then that's all that matters, sir. See you later.'

Biggles went out.

These are other Knight Books

Captain W. E. Johns wrote over eighty books about Biggles, the intrepid airman whose adventures take him and his comrades all over the world.

Many of these books are available, published by Brockhampton Press. Here is a list of the titles available in Knight Books:

BIGGLES AND THE CHINESE PUZZLE
BIGGLES IN THE TERAI
BIGGLES BURIES THE HATCHET
BIGGLES AND THE PLOT THAT FAILED
BIGGLES INVESTIGATES
BIGGLES AND THE NOBLE LORD
BIGGLES IN THE UNDERWORLD
BIGGLES AND THE GUN-RUNNERS
BIGGLES AND THE LITTLE GREEN GOD
BIGGLES AND THE PENTITENT THIEF
BIGGLES AND THE BLACK MASK
BIGGLES SORTS IT OUT
BIGGLES FLIES WEST
BIGGLES SPECIAL CASE
BIGGLES TAKES A HAND
BIGGLES TAKES IT ROUGH
BIGGLES OF THE INTERPOL
BIGGLES AND THE BLUE MOON

These are other Knight Books

Willard Price 'Adventure' stories are all
about Hal and Roger and their amazing
adventures in search of wild animals for the
world's zoos. Here is a complete list of the
adventures available in Knight:

1 AMAZON ADVENTURE
2 SOUTH SEA ADVENTURE
3 UNDERWATER ADVENTURE
4 VOLCANO ADVENTURE
5 WHALE ADVENTURE
6 AFRICAN ADVENTURE
7 ELEPHANT ADVENTURE
8 SAFARI ADVENTURE
9 LION ADVENTURE
10 GORILLA ADVENTURE
11 DIVING ADVENTURE
12 CANNIBAL ADVENTURE

Ask your local bookseller, or at your public
library, for details of other Knight Books, or
write to the Editor-in-Chief, Knight Books,
Arlen House, Salisbury Road, Leicester,
LE1 7QS